The Cartwheel KID

Scott and Jim Upper

scottupper@gmail.com
jimupper4@gmail.com

Original illustrations by Karol Baker
karolart@aol.com

ISBN-13: 978-1475203653
ISBN-10: 1475203659

BISAC: Fiction / Sports

ACKNOWLEDGEMENTS

Special shout-outs to Diana McCauley, Lorelei Dann Noe, Kelly Toy, Vivian Hudson, Jamie Ciferni, Julie Daniels Ciferni, Bill Hiscock, Susanne Shultz, Omar Boyd, Eddy Goldberg, Randy Wilhelm, Rollin Kibbe, Steven O'Brien, Toni Knezevich, and Doug Booher.

Special woof-outs to Boss Upper and the dog parks across the good ole' USA.

PART 01

CHAPTER ONE

From the top of the highest pull-up bar, eleven-year old Pookie Jameson watched the awful, red-haired twins fist-bump each other and jog away like nothing had happened. Yep, the scrawny little freckle-heads pranced over to Big Vernon's bench as if they hadn't just tripped Pookie, clocked him in the side of the head with a rock, and threatened to shoot him with a gun – all because he was short!

The twins sat down on either side of Big Vernon. From Pookie's perch, they looked like gargoyles on a castle wall.

But this was far from a castle. It was a concrete slab in the courtyard of the Vineland Children's Residential Treatment Center: a holding cell for orphans and abused children in South Jersey.

Pookie clamped his ankle around the rusty metal bar for leverage, gently touched his throbbing temple, and examined his palm. *Definitely not blood,* he thought. *But what is this sticky mess?* He rubbed the clear goo onto his thigh and moved some tiny white bits around with his fingertips until it dawned on him. *Egg!*

Pookie felt sick. He wished Cross was still around. *You're pretty fast,* Cross would have said, paying no attention to what had just happened. In fact, he would have probably walked over to Pookie, leaned up against the base, and said something like, *you're so fast that you should play basketball.* Cross had been gone for a whole year. He was the only friend Pookie ever had at the Center. Sure, he was always talking about boring basketball. But still, he was the only halfway decent kid around.

A buzzing sound filled Pookie's head and he bit his lower lip to keep from crying. He shimmied back on the bar, squeezed his knees around it, and lowered himself backwards until he was hanging upside down. Blood rushed to his head. His skull throbbed even harder. Two big tears rolled up his forehead into his shock of blond hair. Pookie sniffed and took one last inverted glance at the gargoyles.

"Pookie!" Counselor Hall shouted from the far side of the yard. "You have a visitor!"

At the sound of Hall's voice, Pookie took one last sniff, pumped his hips, released his legs, arched his back, and yanked his feet around to a thud. A perfect penny drop. "Uncle Albert!" shouted Pookie. He turned a quick cartwheel, and then zipped through between the clump of boys, instantly forgetting about the whole thing.

CHAPTER TWO

Later that day

"Uncle Albert! Uncle Albert!" Pookie yelled as he dogpaddled to the ladder. "Did you see it? I did a flip with a dive at the end! I did a One-and-a-Half! Uncle Albert!"

Pookie crawled out of the pool, rolled over the hot stone gutter, and stood at attention behind Uncle Albert's newspaper. "Just in time, too," he beamed as the whistle blew, indicating the end of the public hour.

"Way to go, Pook," Uncle Albert crumbled the sports page and stood up. "You want a hot dog?"

Pookie turned around to sit on the bottom bench of the metal bleachers. "Ouch! Hot!" He jumped up, walked a couple of steps forward, and stared out at the glistening pool. "How cool was that?" he sighed.

The sound of a bouncing diving board broke Pookie's trance.

**

"Look, Uncle Albert!" Pookie grabbed the approaching hot dog and crammed it into his mouth. "There's a whole team of kid divers over there." Across the pool, at the other set of the diving boards, a clump of kids stood around two one-meter boards. A small boy in a Speedo climbed up onto one board, jumped, and sliced through the water like a shiny new penny. "Man, look at that. That's so easy."

A second kid stood on the end of the board, put his hands over his head, and leaned into a head first dive. A tan man in a nearby lifeguard chair shouted something.

Pookie tapped his uncle on the newspaper that had snuck back up between them. "You could do that," said Uncle Albert as he lowered the paper again.

"I know," Pookie smiled through ketchup lips.

A third kid, this time a girl, jumped off the board, grabbed her knees, and flipped.

"You could do that, too."

"I know!" Pookie threw his hands up and turned a right-side cartwheel. "Why does open dive have to be over already? I want to do more dives!" Like a pendulum, he stopped and turned a left-side cartwheel, slipping a bit on the landing.

"Whoa," said Uncle Albert. "Take it easy, kid." He pushed himself off the bench. As they walked across the deck, the boy looked up at this guy they called his uncle. He wore faded blue jeans and a scratchy knock-off Polo shirt. He didn't know the guy very well, yet he had a faint memory of going to flea markets with him. He must have been very small. Kindergarten-small, even. "Get yer invisible dog collars!" Pookie remembered yelling into the crowd. "Get yer giant sunglasses! Get yer light-up hula-hoops!" Pookie had been through so many horrible things in his young life that he might have forgotten this by now. But the truth of the matter was, he did all of this hollering while jumping up and down on a miniature trampoline. "The tramp is also for sale," he would shout into the crowd, "for the low, low price of nineteen dollars and ninety-nine cents!"

Pookie slapped his feet against the pool deck, one at a time, louder and louder, as they turned the corner. When they reached the straight-away, he lifted his hands up in the air, ready to cartwheel down the deck.

"Don't," Uncle Albert put his hand out in front of Pookie, stopping him just in time. "Wait a minute, Pook."

"Yo," Uncle Albert bellowed up to the man in the raised lifeguard chair. "How much for diving lessons?"

The man in the lifeguard chair wore a straw hat. He also had a blob of silver sunblock on his nose and hairy legs, crossed at the knees.

The man looked angry. Pookie looked down. There was a glob of yellow mustard just to the right of his belly button. Water dripped from the fringes of his cut-off jeans.

"This is a private team," the man in the straw hat sighed. "We only practice here occasionally. We rarely take on new divers. I'm sure you understand." Uncrossing his hairy legs and re-crossing them on the other side, the man turned back to the divers and yelled, "Brittany! Arms higher on the take-off!"

CHAPTER THREE

Pookie wiped the mustard from his belly and looked up at his uncle, who scratched his chin and watched the divers even more intently now. "Listen," he said to the man wearing the straw hat in the lifeguard chair. "Do you think you could just watch the kid do a dive and tell me if he's got any talent? We've been coming here for weeks. He's really into this diving thing."

"Ten meter platform!" the man interrupted. "You're up!" Then he pointed a tanned, hairy finger toward the one-meter diving board and said to Pookie, "Go ahead, kid. You can go after the girl on the tower. Use the inside one-meter board."

Pookie tiptoed across the hot concrete, took two big steps up the short ladder, and walked toward the le of the board. He looked down at the fulcrum wheel. He'd seen the other kids turning the wheel with their feet, so he naturally tried to do the same. But it wouldn't budge. *It's stuck,* he thought. *Or maybe I'm doing it wrong.* He looked around to see if anyone was watching him, but they weren't. Instead, everyone was looking up in the sky.

Pookie looked up too. A small black girl with a bright red bathing cap stood backwards on the highest platform. She bobbed her arms twice, jumped up, and spun around backwards a million times. "Hup!" yelled the man in the straw hat. And just like that, the girl kicked herself out into a straight line and stretched back for the water. Just like that, she disappeared into the blue without a splash.

Pookie's jaw dropped open. He was completely frozen and totally dumbfounded.

"Go already, kid!" whined the girl they called Brittany from somewhere in the water. "What are you waiting for!?"

"Oh, uh-," Pookie shook himself back into the moment and lifted his foot from the fulcrum wheel. "Okay," he said to himself. "Here goes." He took a deep breath and sprinted down the blue plank, making a plan as he went. *I'll take my new trick, the One-and-a-Half, and add another half somersault. Yeah, that's right,* he thought as he raced forward, *this is going to be the fanciest, coolest trick y'all have ever seen. I'm going to spin around so fast that your eyeballs will get all tangled up just watching me. I'm going to do...a DOUBLE SOMERSAULT!*

The board beneath him wobbled as he ran. Near the end, he lifted his feet, punched down like a jackrabbit, and whipped his arms down past his belly.

Centrifugal force pulled his head back as he spun forward into the air. Whoosh! He heard the sound of rushing wind and a flash of white light. *I'm flying!* thought Pookie as his cheeks rippled and stretched back toward his ears, and then WHAM! Out of nowhere, a jarring pain blazed across his chest and shoulders.

Pookie never even made it an inch beneath the surface. Instead, he flopped over like a mackerel and quickly dogpaddled toward the ladder.

Brittany floated between the ladder rails, blocking Pookie's exit. She twirled her long blonde hair in the water and giggled.

Pookie swerved over a few feet and hoisted himself up over the gutter. Then, shuffling over to his uncle, he buried his swollen face into the folds of scratchy shirt.

"C'mon, let's go," said Uncle Albert, tousling the boy's wet hair. They turned away from the team and trudged across the deck. "Those guys are snobs," said Uncle Albert. "Who needs 'em?"

Thankfully, Pookie's One-and-a-Face-Plant was not mentioned again - except once, later that day, when Uncle Albert picked up a drippy orange chicken wing and said, "Hey kid. Listen up. I've got some news that'll make you forget all about that wipeout." He reached up to wipe a bleu cheese smear from his chin but only ended up with a bigger mess, "I made a big score with Smart Phone cases on EBay last month."

"Yeah?" said Pookie, half-heartedly flipping a celery stick into his empty soda cup.

"Yeah, I know it's all pretty boring, kid," continued Uncle Albert. "But this making money stuff only means I won't have to travel so much. It means we'll finally be able to prove a local residence. Which also means-"

Pookie looked up from his plate. "I can live with you?"

"Well, yeah. And possibly even go to school at Bridgeton Middle this fall. I'm still not quite showing enough income for full-time custody, but I'm using the money from the Smartphone score to fund a new idea I just had. If it works, it could be an even *bigger* break for us."

"What's the project?" Pookie said cautiously.

"Well," said Uncle Albert. "There's a new casino opening up in Atlantic City this summer. It's called Big Top. They're building a new pier too, right across the street from it. It's gonna have a bunch of rides, and-"

"Which rides?"

"I don't know, one of those Stand-Up Tilt-a-Majiggies, I think. Oh, I think I also heard them saying something about a Drop Tower."

"A Drop Tower?!" said Pookie. "I love those!"

"Yep. And get this. My old friend BeeBee is one of the principal investors. I pitched an idea to her for a new ride. Sort of a do-it-yourself ride, actually." Uncle Albert leaned forward and whispered across the table, "It involves trampolines."

"Trampolines?!" said Pookie, sitting up straight in his chair.

"Shhh! Shhh! Keep it down. This is top secret! It's a whole floor of 'em, actually. Side by side. Even the walls are gonna be made out of trampolines."

"So, unlimited flying?!" Pookie jumped up and knocked over his empty soda cup and grabbed the celery stick.

"You got it, kid. Unlimited flying."

"You want me to demonstrate?!" said Pookie, flicking the celery stick into a triple flip.

"Yea, kid. I want you to demonstrate. And this time, the other kids can get in on the fun. Fifteen bucks an hour."

"Hmmm," said Pookie. "Not bad. I actually kinda like it. You know, back in the old flea market days, all those kids ever wanted to do was jump on the mini-tramp, anyway. But it was so small."

"Well then, this calls for a toast," said Uncle Albert, holding up a big plastic cup of orange soda. "Atlantic City, here we come."

"Atlantic City," said Pookie, holding up his empty cup. "Here we come!"

Uncle Albert poured half of his orange soda into Pookie's plastic cup. Pookie downed the soda in three big, nose-tickling gulps, put down the cup, and let out his biggest burp to date.

CHAPTER FOUR

Bridgeton, New Jersey

"Hey, Confetta," twelve-year old Tanika Dawn reached into the nest and lifted up her favorite chicken's tail feathers. "Whatcha you got for me today? Ooooh! A couple of big brown doozies! Good job, Miss!"

With an egg in each hand, Tanika swung around on her knees to face the chicken door. She turned a somersault though the cut-out hole, two more down the ramp, and landed at the base of the sawhorse. "Woot!" she yelled as she popped up to her feet, stuffed the eggs into her front pockets, and pressed up into a handstand. Then, stepping down, she threw her hands up in the air, smiled, and waved to an imaginary crowd.

"Tanika!" her mother yelled. "You better bring me them eggs!"

"Harumph," said Tanika as she hopped down onto to the old spare tire. She hoped it would bounce, but it never went anywhere but down flat to the ground. "Oh well," she said, shrugging her shoulders. She skipped across the yard, up the porch, and into the house. "I need a trampoline," she said as she burst into the room. "Can I puleeeze get a trampoline?"

"You'll get a trampoline," said her mother, pulling a steaming pie out of the oven, "when you *earn* a trampoline."

"How am I supposed to *earn* a trampoline," said Tanika, "when there's nobody around here except chickens? Lord knows *they* don't have money!"

"I've already explained this to you, young lady," said Tanika's mother. "Weren't you listening? We're going to start selling chicken pastry out of your Aunt BeeBee's hat shop this week. So it would behoove you to keep those chickens fat and happy".

"Behoove?" Tanika said with a chuckle. "Is that like beehive? Cuz there's a beehive behind the old-"

"Tanika," her mother sighed. "Listen up, girl. Chickens might not have money, but with a little luck and a lot of hard work, we might just be able to turn them into money. Now hand over the eggs."

Tanika reached into her pockets and looked down at the big brown eggs: one in each hand, each with a zig-zag crack. Tanika winced and passed them to her momma. "Tanika!" her mother said angrily shaking off her oven mitts. "You been turning somersaults again?"

CHAPTER FIVE

"Twelve bowls of chicken pastry," said Tanika as she dropped the last of the cling-wrapped goodies onto the top shelf. "Okay, that's it for the chicken pastry."

"Alright, now." said Tanika's mom, holding a clipboard. "Two sweet potato pies."

"One sweet potato pie," said Tanika, pulling a large brown pie from the plastic crate. She scooted it back onto her forearm and grabbed a second pie with her free hand. "Two sweet potato pies."

"Three dozen eggs," said Tanika's mom.

"Three dozen eggs," said Tanika as she put the pies down on the shelf and spun around toward the eggs "Thank you, birds!" she pressed her hands together and bowed her head. Then she grabbed the egg cartons, one at a time, and placed them on the shelf where the pill box hats used to be.

"Six whole chickens," said Tanika's mom. "Dressed and frozen."

"Six whole chickens," said Tanika, swirling around again. "Dressed and-" Tanika froze. There they were, her old friends. The clucking goofballs that made her laugh a thousand times. There they were, plucked, feathered, and hard as ice. "Momma?" said Tanika as she took a step backward. "I- I- can't-"

"Tanika!" Back at the counter, Gramma held up a wrinkly old fist. "I told you, girl. Don't go gettin' all caught up in that head of yours. Just do whatcha do. How're we ever gonna get you pluckin' and drawin' these birds if you can't even put them *away*?"

"Thank you, all you beautiful birds," Tanika whispered as she lifted a frozen chicken from the crate. "Thank you for your sacrifice."

"Tanika!" shouted Gramma, still shaking her fist at the counter. "Ms. Jane Gillette would turn over in her *grave* if she saw you hesitatin' like that!"

"I know," said Tanika as she put the chicken on the middle shelf.

"You know, Jane and Edward grew them chickens and vegetables out at Monticello. And you know what they done did? They done sold it right back to

President Jefferson. And you know what else? Your great great great great great great Gramma, the one and only Ms. Elizabeth Hemings, woulda' told you for exactly how much, 'cuz she ran the whole dang farm in the first pl-"

"Momma, that's enough," said Tanika's mom. "How many times are you gonna tell this story?"

"Well it's important, child," said Tanika's Gramma, "cuz history repeats. And that's what we're gonna do now! Repeat. You see, the landlord? Aunt BeeBee? Well, she done got enough hats. But chicken pastry? Ain't nobody *ever* gonna get enough of our chicken pastry!"

CHAPTER SIX

The new neon sign above the barn door was *supposed* to say:

Aunt BeeBee's Chicken and Hats

But the *and* was broken, so instead, the sign would actually say:

Aunt BeeBee's Chicken Hats

Aunt BeeBee didn't notice the mistake. In fact, she didn't notice the new sign at all, since it was still daylight. She pushed open the heavy barn door.

The bells jangled.

Aunt BeeBee's jewels jangled even louder.

"Aunt BeeBee!" said Tanika as her favorite aunt pranced through the door in a cloud of sweet smelling perfume.

"Hello ladies," Aunt BeeBee said. "What have you got for me today? Something smart? Something chic? Something festive and fun?" Aunt BeeBee spun around like a showgirl, her body squishing out of a tight jeweled dress. And then she suddenly stopped mid-twirl. "Ewww," she scrunched up her nose. "What's that smell?"

"It's food, Aunt BeeBee!" said Tanika. "The groceries from the farm are finally here! Including mama's world famous chicken pastry."

"Hmmm," Aunt BeeBee looked around at the shop. There were crates on the floor and most of the shelves were empty. "Oh yes. I forgot about that. Where're my hats?"

"Over there," said Tanika, pointing to the corner. The hats, which were normally displayed along the wall with plenty of space, were smooshed over onto a corner shelf.

"Hi, sis," said Tanika's mom, giving Aunt BeeBee a peck on the cheek.

"Hi, honey," said Aunt BeeBe, kissing her back, and then "Hi momma," to Gramma, who stood grumpily behind the register.

"So, what's the occasion?" Tanika said as she dove into the hats. "I'm gonna find the perfect hat for you."

"Well, girls," said Aunt BeeBee. "I've got some exciting news. You know the new casino going up in Atlantic City?"

"Sure," said Tanika's mom. "I've seen the billboards. Big Top, right?"

"Yes, that's the one. Well, construction is almost complete on the new pier and Big Top is just about ready to open. And can you guess who the new principal investor is? That's right. Yours truly," Aunt BeeBee threw her hands up in the air, turned around in place, and continued, "The great Aunt BeeBee."

Tanika grabbed an orange polka-dotted hat and turned it around in her hands. "Nope," she said to herself as she put it back down on the shelf.

"Naturally I am in charge of all entertainment," said Aunt BeeBee. "We'll be hosting the Young Miss America Beauty Show later in the fall, and before that, a High Dive exhibition this summer."

"High dive?" said Tanika. "Did you just say *high dive*?"

CHAPTER SEVEN

"Back when I was a little girl," said Aunt BeeBee, "they had a retired racing horse at the old Steel Pier. And a jockey would ride it out off of a platform, straight off the edge into the pool below."

"Oh," Tanika's mom muttered under her breath. "That was just awful. That poor horse."

"People would come from miles and miles away." said Aunt BeeBee as she pranced a few feet further into the shop, leaned over, and checked her lipstick on the reflection of the new freezer door. "It was quite a spectacle."

"A diving horse?" said Tanika as she picked up a wide-brimmed yellow sun hat. "How bizarre."

"Well dear," said Aunt BeeBee. "Apparently they won't allow us work with horses anymore. They say it's cruelty to animals, which I suppose it is-" She paused for a moment, touching a red fingernail to her chin. "But folks sure love the thrill of high diving and they always will. So I figured, why not use *people* instead of horses?"

"Yup," said Tanika, "The Cirque du Soleil water show in Vegas has high divers. Miss Applejack showed us a video in Arts class."

"Ooh child," said Aunt BeeBee. "I like that Miss Applejack. I suppose this will be the New Jersey version of Cirque du Soleil. Maybe we'll call it *Cirque du BeeBee.* Oh, wait'll you see what we're cooking up, ladies. There'll be a clear glass aquarium right smack in the middle of the first floor. Inside, it will have the most exotic fishes from around the world. And three times a day, the alarms will sound, the roof will open, and the aquarium will transform into-"

"A pool to catch the high diver."

"Bingo," said Aunt BeeBee, touching the tip of Tanika's nose. "I like you. You're smart."

"What?!" said Tanika's momma. "Where's the diver coming from?"

"Why, from the top of the ladder, of course," said Aunt BeeBee. "You see, the rooftop is automatic. One touch of a button and it will open to the blue sky above. Another touch and the ladder will extend straight up through the roof. At the top of the ladder, the diver will wave to the people on the boardwalk, the new pier, and beyond."

"That is so cool!" said Tanika. "I wanna-"

"Oh no," said Tanika's mom. "Don't you even *think* about it."

"Aunt BeeBee, you *know* I'm a diver, right?" said Tanika. "You know I practice every day at Vineland Y, right? And summers in Cherry Hill? And you *know* I go to national competitions and everything, right? And that I'm the state champion platform diver. Right?"

"Tanika!" yelled Gramma. "Stop your bragging."

"I'm not!" Tanika spotted a black rim, sticking out from beneath a pink pillbox hat. "I just thought I could bring the Big Top more customers. I've always been good at waving." She raised her hand, cupped her fingers together and turned it side-to-side, like a princess at a parade.

"Just how high *is* this high dive?" said Tanika's mom.

"Oh," said Aunt BeeBee. "It's only-"

"Got it!" Tanika yelled as she dislodged a vintage black top hat from the shelf. The other hats toppled down all around her. "Here it is, Aunt BeeBee! Your new hat!"

"Hmmm," said Aunt BeeBee, squishing her nose. "It looks like it came straight outta some old-fashioned circus."

"Exactly," said Tanika, proudly.

"I love it, child!" said Aunt BeeBee.

"I knew it," said Tanika. "See, mom?" she said, cocking her head from side-to-side. "Not *everybody* thinks I'm lame." She raised her hand again and waved to an imaginary crowd.

"This will do," said Aunt BeeBee as she popped on the top hat, tilted it to one side, and bent over toward the freezer. "Yes, this will do just fine." Then she winked at Tanika's reflection.

Tanika kept turning her hand from left to right, waving, waving, and waving some more.

"Atlantic City," said Aunt BeeBee. "Here we come."

CHAPTER EIGHT

Atlantic City, New Jersey

The summer sun was blasting. Even though it was still morning, thousands of people buzzed about with fresh-whipped cotton candy and mustard covered soft pretzels. The smell of oven-roasted peanuts mixed in and wafted through the crowd and up the steps to the trampoline platform. Pookie stood beside Uncle Albert, breathing in the sweet n' salty goodness.

"Step right up, folks!" Uncle Albert yelled from the top of the steps. "It's the opening day of the Big Top Casino and Peanut Pier."

Uncle Al's *Catch Some Air, Dude!* trampoline park was located half-way down the pier on the right. At the top of the steps, just behind Pookie and Uncle

Albert, was a big blue curtain. "Today's your lucky day!" he shouted to the gathering crowd. "Because behind this curtain is the ninth wonder of the world! That's right folks, it's a man-made miracle. A wonder beyond all wonders."

Pookie shifted his weight from side to side. Gripping the curtain rope with his left hand, he swirled his right hand in the air, giving Uncle Albert's speech a visual aid. It had taken *forever* to get to this moment. Four weeks to dig the hole, two more to set the trampolines in place. Six of the longest weeks of his life. So the stakes were high. And the show was about to begin.

"Not since the Eiffel tower has mankind achieved such an accomplishment," boomed Uncle Albert. Pookie curved his hand up a bit, and then down again in a dramatic gesture. "Not since the Pyramids in Egypt has the human race pulled together to build the unthinkable," bellowed Uncle Albert. Pookie drew a giant triangle. "We once thought that landing a man on the moon was a big deal, well I'll tell you-"

"Okay, okay!" Pookie poked Uncle Albert in his leg. "Get on with it!"

"We, uh," Uncle Albert stumbled on his words, and then said, "Pookie, the rope!"

Pookie gave a sharp tug on the rope and the curtain dislodged itself from the hook in the archway. Whoosh! Heavy folds of fabric fell to each side.

"Behold!" yelled Pookie and Uncle Albert.

The crowd gasped and then went silent.

"Yesssss," hissed a kid in the crowd. "Trampolines."

"That's right, kid!" Uncle Albert said. "Trampolines! Seven wide and seven across. Unlimited flying for only fifteen bucks an hour. Get your wristband at any one of the machines against the far wall. If you're under eighteen, you'll need a parent or guardian with you at the kiosk. "Pookie," said Uncle Albert, pointing at Pookie. "You're on!"

Pookie had already kicked off his left shoe but the laces got all knotted up on the right one. "Arrrgh!" he yelled, jamming one foot into the other. "It's stuck!"

Just as Uncle Albert turned toward him, the shoe popped loose and flung into the air. Uncle Albert reached out, caught it, and set it down at his feet. "Ta Da!" he yelled, pretending that this was all part of the act. The crowd laughed.

Pookie's heart thumped faster than ever. He took two quick steps back, turned around, and hopped onto the front middle trampoline.

Though he only got to jump around once, he'd choreographed his performance perfectly in his mind. There'd be a single bounce on each trampoline. As he made his way to the back, he'd jump higher and higher, clearing each of the seven blue spring covers. Finally, at the diagonal trampoline in the back, he'd do a 180 degree turn and start bouncing back toward the crowd. Only on his way back, he'd do a flip on each trampoline.

The crowd roared as Pookie cleared first one, two, then three blue spring covers! His forehead wrinkled and his tongue slipped out in urgent concentration. He prepared for the turn. He heard someone in the crowd scream, "Look at that kid!" which popped an image in his brain: the bellyflop at the Y. The famous double that only ended up as a One-and-a-Face Plant. *I will not under-rotate,* he thought, frantically. *I will not under-rotate.*

"Four, five, six, seven!" Pookie counted out loud as his eyes darted between the far wall up ahead and the black mats beneath his feet. When he finally reached the end, he bounced off the diagonal trampoline, and turned around to face the crowd. Then he flipped. And flipped. And flipped again. The crowd roared.

I will not under-rotate. I will not under-rota- By the fourth flip, something was terribly wrong. Pookie had over-compensated and was tilted forward on each landing. *I'm over-rotating! I'm over-rotating!* Pookie's brain screamed as he whipped forward, each somersault more out-of-control than the last.

To the untrained eye, Pookie was flipping nicely along. But in reality, Pookie wasn't sure that he could ever *stop* flipping. "Five, six, seve-"

Wham!

The lights went out on Pookie Jameson.

CHAPTER NINE

"Pookie!" said Uncle Albert. "Pookie!"

"Huh?" he said, staring at a triangle of spinning Uncle Albert heads. "Uncle Albert?"

"Oh thank God!" Uncle Albert scooped up Pookie and plopped him onto his feet. "How many fingers am I holding up, kid?"

"Umm," Pookie saw a kaleidoscope of hands. "Twenty-five?"

"You're okay, kid." Uncle Albert touched Pookie's cheeks and forehead. "You're okay."

While all this was happening, a dozen kids pushed and shoved their way up the stairs, flashing their green wristbands at Uncle Albert. "Green, you have 'til two o'clock," Uncle Albert said to the first kid. "No double bouncing. No tricks near the entrance."

He pulled Pookie swiftly to his side. “Green, you have ‘til two o’clock,” he continued. “Green, you have ‘til two o’clock-”

Pookie slid down Uncle Albert’s leg. When he reached the floor, he slumped forward with his legs flared out to the sides.

“Good thing you broke that fall with your arms, kid,” said Uncle Albert. “And a *real* good thing your shoe was there. Coulda been a lot worse. Green, you have ‘til two o’clock. Green, you have ‘til-”

Pookie picked up his smooshed shoe and turned it over in his hands. Tiny clear stars danced around the laces. “Green……you……… have……….’til…………two…….o’clock……. Green…………….you…………have…-” Uncle Albert’s voice seemed to be in slow-motion as it faded into the click-clack of the Drop Tower and the whir of the Stand-Up Tilt-A-Majiggy. And then, emerging from somewhere beneath the carnival sounds, Pookie heard a lady’s voice. It came from far away, but even so, her words were clear and bright. “Ladies and gentlemen!” she said. “Step right up and step right to the Big Top Casino, because in one hour from now is the soon-to-be world famous Big Top high dive!”

Pookie hoisted himself onto his knees, crawled between Uncle Albert's legs, and scrambled to the steps.

"Kid!" said Uncle Albert as he yanked Pookie back by the belt. "You're delirious! You can't go anywhere! Your nose is all swollen! You just blacked out!"

"But it's the high di-" But as soon as he opened his mouth, something snapped. From deep inside Pookie's head came a tidal wave of pain. And instead of holding back, Pookie let out a scream. A scream so loud that all the green wrist-banders stopped mid-bounce and turned their heads. A scream so loud that Aunt BeeBee, who was still announcing the Big Top high dive, took off her black top hat and marched across the street toward Peanut Pier.

CHAPTER TEN

"What on Earth is going on here?" Aunt BeeBee said to Jimbo, Peanut Pier's head security guard. "I heard a scream. And this was no *I'm scared 'cuz I'm free-fallin' on the Drop Tower* scream. This was clearly a *Help me - I'm in pain!* scream."

"Well, there *was* a little accident," said Jimbo. "Albert's kid flipped onto the platform. Landed on his shoe, though. Close call. Coulda' been worse."

"Where's the boy now?" she said with tight, pursed lips. "Is he hurt?"

"Well," said George, "Actually I don't know. I mean, I put my hand on his shoulder, but he just slipped right out and disappeared into the crowd."

“BeeBee! It’s a success!” said Uncle Albert as his old friend BeeBee stepped up to his platform. “Look at all of the happy bouncers!”

“Where’s the kid?” said Aunt BeeBee. “I heard he was hurt.”

“He’s, uh-” Uncle Albert said, looking all around. “Um-”

Aunt BeeBee scanned the pier, then looked back at the trampolines. “I’m not seeing helmets. I thought you were going to be providing helmets, Albert.”

“I know, BeeBee,” said Uncle Albert. “Trust me, I know. They’re on order from China. I’m not happy about the delay either. I mean, jeez, every hour they are late is costing me money! Without helmets, wrist guards, and shoe rentals, I’ll *never* make the rent, much less enough money to get a permanent address so that I can get custody of-” He stopped and shouted the boy’s name into the crowd, “Pookie!”

“Look Albert,” said Aunt BeeBee. “I know we go way back. And I *do* think it’s very noble that you want to adopt Pookie. And I truly hope that happens, for his sake as well as yours. But business is business. You *must* make the rent.”

**

The Drop Tower was, to date, the tallest ride in history. During the testing phase, Pookie watched as the bright yellow bench was slowly lifted to the top of the structure. Then it would be released, free-falling 110 meters before the hydraulic brakes kicked in. Two long, slow bounces at the bottom later, the bench would come to rest.

Last week, each of the Australian ride crew members had to tell Pookie that he could not go on the ride.

"The ride's not open yet, kid." said one.

"But the chair's empty!" yelled Pookie as he cartwheeled away.

"You're too short, mate," said another. "You might slip out."

"Bull pucky!" yelled Pookie as he cartwheeled away.

"We wouldn't want you to get hurt, mate," said a third.

"Lamest reason ever!" yelled Pookie as he cartwheeled away.

But today, the ride was open, and while all three of the Australian carnies were busy strapping people down into the chair, Pookie snuck around to the backside.

His face throbbed as he shielded his eyes and looked up at the sky-high ride. Even though there were no bullies chasing him, Pookie knew he had to climb - up, up, and away. He had a quick flash memory of the pull-up bar at the Center. He took a deep breath and whispered, “Easy-peasy, Japaneezy” to himself. Then, one rung at a time, he carefully wedged his feet into the angled beams, grabbing crossbar after crossbar for leverage.

Up he climbed, into the bright blue sky, only looking down once during his ascent. It was a big mistake, too. He got so dizzy that he imagined losing his balance and tumbling down the center of the tower, banging his swollen nose on every bar! After that, he decided that it would be best to look up in the direction he was going, picturing each section as its own pull-up bar, at least until he got to where he was going.

CHAPTER ELEVEN

From his secret spot on a plank, halfway up the Drop Tower, Pookie finally felt secure enough to look down. From way up in the sky, Aunt BeeBee and Uncle Albert looked like little ants. Next to them, twenty fleas hopped about on little black patches. "Look," he yelled into the salty air. "A genuine flea circus!"

Just in front of the pier, a big brown beetle - no, wait - a delivery van – pulled up. The driver unloaded a carton and placed it on the boardwalk. Then he unloaded another. And another. Pookie knew exactly what the boxes were: helmets, wrist-guards, and special trampoline shoes. He had to get down and help Uncle Albert set up. But not yet!

Just across the boardwalk, up in the sky, there was a big slab of concrete with a patch of round steel in the middle – the Big Top rooftop. “Cool,” Pookie said to himself as he shifted around on the plank. “That must be where the high dive ladder comes out.”

The Drop Tower started to rumble. As the first yellow bench slowly click-clacked up to the Drop Tower base, he grabbed the beams on either side of him. He turned his head slightly to the left, just enough to see three sets of dangling legs. “Lucky ducks,” he said. Then he looked back at the Big Top rooftop and waited.

**

Inside the Big Top Casino, Tanika swiftly climbed up the ladder. When she reached the top, just below the ceiling, she released one hand and signaled down to the casino manager, Chuck Trawley.

“Ladies and gentlemen!” announced Chuck. “Please direct your attention to the center of the room!”

A few people raised their heads from their slot machines and roulette wheels. The others, hidden inside clouds of cigarette smoke, continued to gamble. “This aquarium,” said Chuck as he carried the microphone around the perimeter, “is filled with exotic fishes from around the world. Some of them are dangerous. Some of them are not. This ladder," he said, tapping the microphone on the metal beams that climbed up the side of the glass, is the base of the high dive ladder. Ladies and gentlemen, please direct your eyes straight up the ladder!"

From Tanika's vantage point, the aquarium was a shimmering pool. There were little fluffy clouds here and there, and people with cotton candy and soda-pops streaming in from the boardwalk entrance. Tanika opened her hand, and then closed it sharply into a fist, the cue for Chuck Trawley to push three buttons. The first button would open the mechanical rooftop. The second would send a pulse through the water that would, in turn, cause the fish to swim to the outer edges. The third would extend the ladder straight up through the roof, high into the sky above the casino.

Chuck Trawley pushed the first button. The motor engaged and the roof spiraled open from the center. A thick column of sunlight beamed down, flooding the aquarium with light.

Chuck pushed the second button. The fish swam to the sides of the glass tank.

Chuck pushed the third button. The ladder slowly extended into the sky. Tanika took a deep breath and gripped the bars with both hands. Once above the roof, the cool ocean breeze washed over her, along with the sound of seagulls and carnival music. She tried to keep her eyes glued to the top rung, but Atlantic City was just too exciting from this angle. First off, there were a million ant-sized people on the boardwalk. Beyond that, Peanut Pier bustled with the same little ants lined up in front of three attractions: a Stand-Up Tilt-A-Whirl, *Catch Some Air, Dude!* trampoline park, and a Drop Tower. Beyond the rides, a big blue ocean stretched on forever.

The dive ladder came to a halt, and Tanika glanced down at her target: a small black circle. She felt a gust of wind on her back, wobbled a little, and took a deep breath.

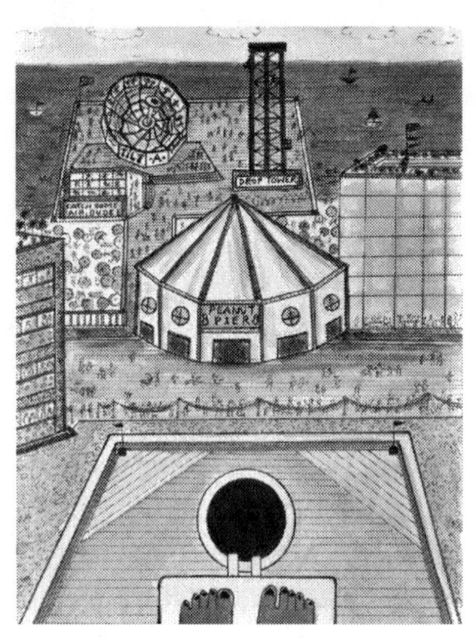

CHAPTER TWELVE

"Aaaaahhhhh!" Three screaming teenagers whizzed down the side of the Drop Tower, just a few feet away from Pookie. But he was fixated on the little black girl with the red bathing cap that had just risen high into the bright blue Jersey sky. "Put a cork in it!" he shouted into the back of the screaming, dropping bench. "The high diver is about to go!"

"Ladies and Gentlemen of the Atlantic City Boardwalk!" Aunt BeeBee announced into the microphone, "If you look high into the sky, way above the Big Top Casino, you will see the one and only, death defying Tanika Dawn!"

Tanika looked to her right and then to her left. On either side of her was a parking garage that reached up eight stories. Cars and trucks were parked on every level. On the top floor, three teenagers leaned over the guard rail, chanting, "Jump! Jump! Jump!"

"Okay, okay," Tanika whispered as another gust of wind blew, this time making the ladder sway. "Give me a second, will ya?" Tanika reached behind her back with both hands and clutched the ladder. She wiggled her toes and took a deep breath of salty air. "On the count of three," she said to herself. "One. Two-"

Back across the sky, Pookie bit his lower lip as he watched the girl grab the ladder behind her back. She waved, first to the right and then to the left. And then, suddenly, she looked straight out in front of her, hopped off of the tiny square, and arched back toward the ladder with her arms spread out to the sides. The girl fell five stories in a perfectly straight position, pulled her legs into a loose tuck, and kicked out, just short of vertical. "Holy guacamole!" he yelled as she disappeared into the black hole. "What the-?! How the heck did she?!?" Pookie banged on the bars like an animal in a cage.

On the top of the parking garage, the teenagers whooped and whistled. People on the boardwalk hollered too. They pointed up to the sky asking, each other "Did you see that?! Did you see that?!"

How was that even possible? thought Pookie. He scratched his chin and watched the ladder slowly retract down through the hole. *How did she time it so that one somersault fit perfectly into a twenty meter drop? Heck, I couldn't even stop a flip on the trampoline!*

**

By the time Pookie got back to *Catch Some Air, Dude!,* Uncle Albert was opening the last box. "Hey kid," he said. "Where've you been? How's your face?"

"It's okay," said Pookie. "A ladder came out of the casino and the high diver dove off of it. She went right through the roof. Can we watch it from inside next time? Please? I really want to see where she lands."

"Tell you what," said Uncle Albert as he put down the box knife and inspected Pookie's nose and chin. "You help me get these helmets organized and I'll have Rory cover us while we bop over for the next show."

"It's a deal," Pookie said, reaching into the box. "Kid's medium," he said as he quickly grabbed two bright blue helmets. "Adult small."

"Whoa, slow down," said Uncle Albert. "One at a time. Don't worry, little man. We've got an hour before the next high dive. Hang those on the fence by the chinstraps, will ya'?"

**

When the hour was almost up, Uncle Albert led Rory over to the trampoline entry point. “It’s just about three o’clock now, Rory,” he said. “Most of the bouncers peter out before their hour is up, so you probably won’t have to worry about kicking anybody off. Just keep your eye on the black wrist-banders. We want to make sure they get in at three.”

“No cake,” said Rory. “Piece o’ sweat.”

**

“Ladies and Gentlemen!” Aunt BeeBee stood on the steps of the Big Top Casino in her black top hat. “Step right up! It’s the moment you’ve been waiting for! Tanika Dawn’s death defying high dive!”

“Come on!” said Pookie as he tugged on Uncle Albert’s arm as they weaved through Peanut Pier and across the crowded boardwalk.

CHAPTER THIRTEEN

As they approached the steps to the casino entrance, Aunt BeeBee tipped her top hat. Then she turned around and wiggled her backside. Pookie giggled.

Once inside the casino, Uncle Albert led Pookie across the red and gold carpet. Hand in hand, they walked between two rows of slot machines and up two steps to the giant glass tank. "Sweet," said Pookie. He reached up and put his hand on the cool glass. A lionfish swam up and looked out at him, his long brown spikes jutting out in every direction.

"Well well well, if it isn't the great fish killer of 2007!" said Chuck Trawley as he slapped Albert on the back. "I thought you were still doing time for murder."

"What's he talking about, Uncle A?"

"Oh, please. Look who's talkin'!" barked Uncle Albert. "Your high diver's gonna land in this tank and make sushi out of these fish!"

"Your uncle, young man," said Chuck, "is a brilliant businessman. Always with the latest and greatest. But he can't resist a new gimmick. Back in '07, he ordered a thousand necklaces that had actual, live fish in them. But all the fish were dead in a day, my friend. Dead in a day. Made the whole boardwalk smell like-"

"Oh for Pete's sake," said Uncle Albert. "At least I never had a minor diving through a rooftop into a fish tank with poisonous-"

"Ladies and Gentleman," Chuck interrupted, holding up a finger to silence Uncle Albert. "Please direct your attention center of the room. This aquarium is filled with exotic fishes from around the world. Some of them are dangerous. Some of them are not. This ladder is the base of the high dive ladder. Ladies and gentlemen, please direct your eyes straight up the ladder!"

Tanika stood at the top of the ladder and closed her hand into a fist.

Chuck Trawley pushed the first button. The steel roof spiraled open, and sunlight flooded the tank.

He pushed the second button and a low, pulsing sound filled the tank. All the fishes swam to the outer edges of the glass.

He pushed the third button and the ladder extended up through the roof. Tanika disappeared into the sky.

"Ladies, gentlemen," Chuck Trawley announced as he patted Pookie on the head. "and honored guests of the Big Top Casino, we have cameras on the high diver for your viewing pleasure. If you look up at the bar monitors, you will see three different views what is happening right now, through the eyes of a young girl that is about to fall twenty meters and land inside of this tank."

The folks that had gathered around the aquarium strained to see the screens that flickered away with grainy images. One angle was from the parking garage. From there, it looked like a gust of wind could just come right up and blow her out to sea. The second angle was from above, looking down past her red bathing cap and the tips of her painted toes, down at the black circle on the roof.

"Oh my God!" screamed a woman with a beehive hairdo.

"It's okay, lady!" yelled Pookie. "I saw her do it earlier and-"

"Three cherries!" the woman screamed over what sounded like a waterfall of metal chunks. "I just won five hundred dollars!"

Splash!

Pookie whipped his head around, just in time to see a little missile shooting through the fish tank with a trail of bubbles. And then, with her red bathing cap still perfectly intact, Tanika Dawn flutter-kicked to the surface, popped over the side of the aquarium, and stepped down the ladder, one foot at a time.

"Holy ravioli," Pookie said to himself as Chuck held out a towel for Tanika. Then he looked around at the audience and said, "You guys should see it from the Drop Tower," he said. "Way better."

CHAPTER FOURTEEN

"See that corner over there?" Uncle Albert said, just after closing time.

"Yeah," said Pookie, only half paying attention as he bounced around in the dark.

"Well, be careful. There's a hole. I took a spring out in the corner. I'll be storing the wrist guards and shoes down below. So whatever you do, don't step *there.*"

"Okay," Pookie turned in mid-air and started bouncing toward the back. "One, two, three, four, five, six, seven! Turn. One, two, three, four, five, six-"

"Seven," said Uncle Albert as Pookie collapsed into a sloppy butt-drop on the trampoline beneath his feet. "C'mon, cuckoo bird. Help me out with these boxes."

"How'd we do today?" said Pookie, catching his breath.

"Very good," said Uncle Albert. "Considering we only had rental gear for the last two sessions. I'd say it was a promising start to the season."

"So, if we did this good every day, maybe we could-"

"Yep," said Uncle Albert. "If we did this good every day, we'd have a nice little nest egg in the fall. Definitely enough for a first month's rent and a security deposit."

"You know," Pookie said as held down the flap of the last cardboard box. "I think that would be just genius."

Uncle Albert chuckled and stretched tape across the gap.

"Can I have a jump?" A small black girl in USA Diving sweat pants appeared out of nowhere.

"Sorry little lady," said Uncle Albert. "We're all closed up for the night."

"I know what I'm doing," said Tanika.

"Uncle A," Pookie shoved an elbow into his uncle's side, "That's Tanika Dawn, the high diver. She knows what she's doing."

"I don't care *who* she is," said Uncle Albert as he squeezed a towel into his duffel bag. "The kiosks are closed. Come back tomorrow, pay the money, fill out the waivers, and then you can bounce. I'm sorry, little lady, it's been a long day. And those are the rules."

"Pookie," said Uncle Albert as he hiked the duffel bag over his shoulder. "Make sure nobody gets on the trampolines. I'm going to get the car. I'll be back in a minute for the final lock-up."

CHAPTER FIFTEEN

"Again!" yelled Tanika as she punched down on the trampoline with her foot, just before Pookie's feet hit the mat. "This time keep your legs straight!"

Pookie was catching twice as much air as normal. So he spread his legs out to the sides. "What the heck?" he yelled into the night sky. "I'm not a cheerleader!" He touched his ankles and returned them to center, just in time for another double-bounce from Tanika.

"You said you wanted to be a diver," said Tanika as he rocketed back up. "You gotta start with the basics. Now tuck!"

"Wahoooo!" yelled Pookie. His legs shook and flailed to the side.

“You gotta think faster than that, kid!” Tanika said as she punched the mat again. “This ain’t no Simon Says! Now Pike!”

Pookie bent his knees and touched the tops of his feet. “Ungggh!”

“Better. Now keep your legs straight,” shouted Tanika. “Again!”

“Ungggh!” Pookie kept his legs straight but his fingers didn’t make it anywhere near his toes.

“Okay, now stop!”

Pookie bent his knees and wobbled to a stop. “I taught myself that trick yesterday!” He laughed.

“Looks like it,” Tanika chuckled while Pookie caught his breath and fidgeted.

“Okay, my turn,” said Tanika. “*You* double bounce *me*.”

Pookie switched places with Tanika.

Tanika did two perfect, soaring bounces. On the third, Pookie pounded his foot onto the trampoline. Her body halted unnaturally on the mat. “No. Punch it *before* I land,” she said, standing still. “That was too late. You’re gonna blow out my knees like that.”

“Oh,” said Pookie. “Okay.”

“Forget-it forget-it,” she said, almost to herself. “We better not do that. Let’s see. What can I teach you?” She stood on the trampoline and looked into the night sky. "Okay, I got it. Now whatever you do, *don't* double-bounce me this time. I'm gonna show you something cool. This is called the triple threat: back flip, back flip, back double."

"You're gonna do a back double?" said Pookie. "In the dark?"

"Yeah, we do doubles a lot," said Tanika as she swung her arms and bounced. "They're lead-ups for back-two-and-a-halfs."

Pookie really didn't care so much about the super-advanced details, or competition dives for that matter. He was, however completely awe-struck. This was already the best trick he'd ever seen, and she hadn't even done it yet.

"One," said Tanika as she effortlessly lifted her straight legs into an open pike and flipped around to vertical. "Two," she said as she launched into a second somersault. "Triple threat!" she yelled as she lifted her legs in front of her face again, wrapped her arms around them, and spun into a back double. When she landed, she put her hands on her hips, and said, "See? It's easy!"

"Easy my pooper," said Pookie.

"Well, I better go," said Tanika. "My Aunt BeeBee's probably lookin' for me." She turned to take a step toward the platform, when-

"Aiiiy!" Tanika yelped as she dropped down into the hole in the corner.

"Oh no!" said Pookie. "Are you okay?"

"I'm okay. I'm okay," she said quickly as she crawled out of the hole. "Stuff like this happens all the time."

"Are you sure?" said Pookie. "That sounded like it-"

"Really," Tanika said, her USA Diving sweatpants ripped down the side and her voice shaking. "I'll be fine." She walked off into the darkness, clutching her arm.

CHAPTER SIXTEEN

"You ready, kid?" said Uncle Albert as he replaced the spring and lowered the blue guard.

"Uh, yeah," said Pookie. But really, he had been pacing along the edge of the platform for the last ten minutes, trying to decide if he should tell Uncle Albert about Tanika's accident. A long time ago, his mom told him not to lie. But is *not saying what happened* the same as lying? Heck, he didn't know. He decided to put it out of his mind for now. Instead, he thought about Tanika's Triple Threat. Whiz bang boom. Magic.

**

The next day, Pookie stood by the trampolines and stared at Uncle Albert's cell phone clock as it slowly ticked its way to noon. *What will Tanika do today*, he thought to himself. *A reverse double?!* Heck, if she could do a back double on the trampoline, she could certainly do a reverse double from the high dive.

"Attention all blues," Pookie shouted through the megaphone. "Time's up! Exit here! If you've got rental shoes, wrist guards, or helmets, you can return them to Rory over there. "Uncle A!" Pookie shouted, "I'm gonna go watch the high dive! Okay?"

"Are the blues off?" yelled Uncle Albert as he held back a crowd of yellows."

"Affirmative!" shouted Pookie as he sprinted through the crowd toward the Drop Tower, turning a cartwheel or two along the way.

**

Up on his little square inside the Drop Tower, Pookie grabbed a handful of peanuts from his pocket. Without taking his eyes off the Big Top rooftop, he popped one into his mouth. "Aaack!" He stuck out his tongue, pinched away the shell bits, and flicked them into the air.

Pookie stared at the black circle. He waited and waited. He grabbed another peanut from his pocket, cracked it open, and looked up again. Nothing was happening. No Aunt BeeBee in a top hat. No Tanika.

The Drop Tower car click-clacked up beside him.

Still nothing.

The Drop Tower bench (and dangling legs) zoomed down.

Still nothing.

After the last peanut was gone and the shell was sufficiently launched into the sky, he smacked his lips together and thought about lemonade, or wait - even better - snow cones.

A second Drop Tower car whizzed down beside him, and then a third. Finally, Pookie gave up and started his long climb down the Drop Tower. Time was probably up for the yellow wrist-banders. Besides, now he couldn't stop thinking about snow cones.

CHAPTER SEVENTEEN

The Stand-Up Tilt-A-Whirl was spinning in its most bizarre position of all: the diagonal. Pookie chomped down on a blue snow cone and watched. Kids and adults of all shapes and sizes had their backs up against the red mats, screaming their heads off.

Pookie liked the Stand-Up-Tilt-A-Whirl okay, but he didn't like the way his hands would slam against the mat when he tried to wave to Uncle Albert. Gravity is weird.

On his way back to *Catch Some Air, Dude!*, Mr. Peanut reached out a big white glove and dropped a handful of salty peanuts into Pookie's hands. Pookie wondered if Mr. Peanut recognized him from before because he'd had a lot of peanuts already.

As Pookie made his way up to the trampoline platform, he was surprised to see that - instead of the usual bouncing frenzy - instead of Rory and Uncle Albert cheerfully passing out wrist bands and rental helmets - the trampolines were roped off and completely empty and Rory was quietly packing a bag.

Behind Rory, Chuck Trawley stood with his arms crossed.

In the far corner, Uncle Albert argued with Aunt BeeBee. "No. No. No," Aunt BeeBee shook her head. "I'm sorry, Albert. My hands are tied on this one. You simply cannot open the trampolines again today and probably not again at all this season." She turned away, and then back again. "Really, Albert I'm sorry. There's nothing I can do."

Chuck Trawley extended his arm to escort Aunt BeeBee down the steps. The two of them disappeared into the crowd.

A blue-lipped Pookie waited until they were gone before he slowly started walking up the steps to the platform. "Pookie!" shouted Uncle Albert, even before he got to the top step. "We're being shut down!"

PART 02

CHAPTER EIGHTEEN

One month later – Bridgeton Middle School

"Come on, Travis!" Tanika said as she held her elbow cast over her lunch tray. "I'd like to eat my mashed potatoes at some point."

Travis looked up, adjusted his glasses, hunched back down, and continued to sign her cast.

"You don't want that cookie, do you?" said Cross, reaching over Tanika's cast for the steal.

"Cut it out," Tanika laughed as she reached over with her good hand and batted Cross' hand away. She was glad school was back in session. Ever since the trampoline accident in Atlantic City, she'd been stuck at the farm, unable to do anything but deliver eggs from the coop to the kitchen.

"'Be not afraid of greatness!'" Danielle read Travis' quote. "'Some are born great, some achieve greatness, and some have greatness thrust upon them'. Wow, Travis. Great quote!"

"Don't look at *me*," said Travis. "*I* didn't make it up."

"Shakespeare?" said Cross.

"Forsooth!"

"Thanks, Travis," Tanika said into her juice box.

"How long you gotta wear that thing?" said Cross.

"Three more weeks," said Tanika. "Then I've got at least two more weeks in physical therapy before I can get back into the water. Coach Dickerson is *not* pleased."

"I hope you learned your lesson, young lady," Travis said in his best old lady voice.

"Don't push it, Travis," said Tanika. "You already took up half of my cast." She turned her cast toward Danielle. "Wanna sign it, D?"

"Sure," said Danielle. She grabbed the pen, scribbled down a quote, and put the pen back on the table.

"What's it say, Cross?"

"'The show must go on'. Lame, Danielle. How's she supposed to dive with a busted elbow?"

"Actually," Travis said to the table. "The quote is very appropriate for Tanika's situation this summer. Did you know that this is actually a shorter version of a longer quote? 'The show must go on, otherwise we'll have to give them their money back!'"

"Yeah, well," said Tanika. "My high dive show was free. It's the *Catch Some Air, Dude!* trampoline guys that had the real problems. Talk about giving your money back. My Aunt BeeBee was forced to shut them down on the first day. So the show *couldn't* go on. I felt really bad. The whole thing was my fault, really. I wonder what ever happened to that kid, anyway. Pookie was his name. Pookie and Uncle Albert."

"Pookie?" said Cross. "From Vineland?!"

"I don't know *where* he was from," said Tanika. "All I know is that he was some crazy little white boy that wanted to be a diver."

"Well," said Cross. "Pookie from Vineland is the only white kid named Pookie that *I've* ever met. I bet it's him. You said he was short, right? He got picked on a lot at the Center for being short. Man, that kid could run. And climb! Those bullies would chase him and he'd scramble up the pull-up bars like a monkey. I'm tellin' ya. Pookie was my home boy!"

CHAPTER NINETEEN

Vineland Residential Treatment Center

"His name's Pookie," said Mrs. Moore. "That's what they call him here at the Center, anyhow." She stared across her desk at Cross' foster parents, Mr. and Mrs. Richardson. "His real name's Scott," continued Mrs. Moore. "Scott Jameson. He's had a real rough go of it. He's spent most of his life in orphanages. He stays with his Uncle Albert sometimes."

"Uncle Albert?" said Mrs. Richardson.

"Yes, an old friend of his deceased father. But Uncle Albert just can't seem to meet the qualifications. There was talk of Uncle Albert adopting Pookie and moving to Bridgeton this year, but it all fell through."

"How come?" said Mr. Richardson.

"Business matters."

Mrs. Richardson wrung her hands.

"Anyway," continued Mrs. Moore. "It's an especially crucial time for the boy. Albert had to leave town and Pookie is all alone again. And suffering. If you take him now, you could very well be saving his life."

"Honestly," said Mrs. Richardson. "That poor boy." She took a sip of water from a small, paper cup. "But Mrs. Moore," she sighed. "I don't see how we can possibly take on another child. There's simply not enough room in the house."

"But Cross has been doing so well," said Mrs. Moore. "I've been hearing so many good things from his teachers. He's reading. He's got a good chance of getting on the basketball team. He-"

"Well, we are certainly enjoying Cross," said Mr. Richardson, in his deep, rough voice. And giving him a little brother might complete the picture." He turned and grabbed his wife's hand. "Don't you think so, mum?"

"But Cliff," said Mrs. Richardson.

"Oh come on now, mum," said Mr. Richardson. "You didn't think we could have gotten off that easy, did you? You didn't think we could have come all this way today without seeing another boy."

"I suppose not," said Mrs. Richardson, almost cracking a smile. "Mrs. Moore, we'd like to meet Pookie. Cross has mentioned him at least a dozen times. We should at least meet him."

"Wonderful," said Mrs. Moore as she walked over to the door and turned the knob. "Counselor Hall," she said into the hallway. "Can you please bring Pookie Jameson to my office."

A few minutes later, Counselor Hall led Pookie down the hall and into Mrs. Moore's office. "There ya' go, kid," he said, releasing his shoulder.

"Hi," said Pookie, staring down at the floor.

"Pookie," said Mrs. Moore. "This is Mr. and Mrs. Richardson."

"He held out a small, weak hand and said, "Nice to meet you, Mr. Richardson."

"Young man," Mr. Richardson grabbed Pookie's hand with his own big, bumpy hand. Then he squeezed it hard and said, "How'd you like to visit your old pal Cross?"

"Cross?" said Pookie, remembering the best friend he ever had. He looked back and forth between all three adults. "You guys know where he is?"

“Why, yes,” said Mrs. Richardson. She looked over at Mrs. Moore, and then down at Pookie. “He’s at our house,” she said, folding her hands on her big, broad lap.

Mr. Richardson patted Pookie on the head like he was a puppy.

“We’ll have to install bunk beds,” Mrs. Richardson said as she put the empty cup on Mrs. Moore’s desk, “and in the summer, when our own boys get back from college, well, we’ll just make it work.”

CHAPTER TWENTY

When the Bridgeton Middle School buzzer went off, the students in Mrs. Polk's sixth grade class sprung from their seats. All but one.

Pookie Jameson sat at his desk, fingers tapping against his knees. He'd spent his entire day in total confusion, and this end-of-the-day buzzer moment was no different. At the Center, the buzzer meant somebody was in serious trouble. Lockdown, even. Pookie stared straight ahead with big wide eyes. Ten seconds after the last student finally left the classroom, he finally stood up.

"You're gonna be just fine, Pookie," said Mrs. Polk as he reached over and slid his books off the desk and onto his hip. "Just fine."

"I know," he said.

Cross had told him to meet by the old oak tree after school, but he wasn't sure where that was. He thought about asking Mrs. Polk where it was, but then he decided that he would find it on his own.

Pookie finally made it out the door and into the hall, where he was swept up in a stampede. As the entire student body moved decidedly toward the back of the building, Pookie bounced around like a pinball. First he bumped into a pointy elbow. Then he scraped against a metal locker. Finally, he banged into a drinking fountain before spinning through the back doors.

Behind the school, the students were dotted and clumped all over the yard. A hundred feet away, there were three folding tables on the grass. An *After School Activities* banner hung above them, stretched between two big oak trees.

"Well, there are the trees, I suppose," said Pookie. "Now where the heck is Cro-"

Wham! In an instant, Pookie was face down in the grass, pinned down by a branch.

"New kid! New kid!" somebody screamed.

Pookie's arms and legs were splayed out to the sides. His books poked into his ribcage from beneath his belly. Sticks scratched his neck and scalp. And then, as quickly as it happened, the leaves around his head rustled, and the branch sprung up and away.

Pookie pushed himself up to his knees and shook the leaves from his hair. He looked to the right and the left and then straight up at a tree branch bobbing in the afternoon sky. He heard a snickering laughter and looked back over to his left. Over by the tree's thick trunk, four kids stood on a bench.

Pookie looked at the kids, then up at the branch again, and suddenly it made sense. Those kids had jumped off the bench, grabbed a branch, and pulled it down on top of him. And the worst part was - the kid on the far side was Cross!

"Again!" yelled the girl next to Cross.

"Whoa. Whoa. Whoa," said Cross. "Enough, guys. That's my brother. Let him get up. Let him go."

"Your *brother*?!"

"Yeah," Cross said cautiously eyeballing the kids.

Pookie picked up the last of his dirt-smudged textbooks and trudged across the grass snorting back a few tears as he walked "Buttwipes," he muttered. "Didn't even give me a chance to-"

"New kid! New kid!" Pookie flinched and ducked his head down, but nothing happened. No branch. No leaves. Still standing. He casually looked around to see if anybody witnessed his false alarm spaz-attack. Nope. Safe.

From somewhere behind him, there was a squeal, a whoop, and some snickering. *Another one bites the dust,* thought Pookie. *Poor sap.*

CHAPTER TWENTY-ONE

At the first table, each clipboard had a sign-up sheet with the club name at the top: Basketball, Flag Football, and Track. Pookie paused, sighed, and looked around. Behind the second table, a black girl in a white T-shirt and a ponytail pinned a poster against the tree. *Bridgeton Swimming and Diving* was sprawled across her back, in black stenciled letters.

"Bridgeton Swimming and Diving? What the-" Pookie lugged his book over to the second table. He looked down at the clipboards: Field Hockey, Swimming, and Soccer. The girl by the tree turned around to grab a second poster from the table, and that's when Pookie saw her face and her arm cast. *Holy block-a-goalie!* he thought to himself. *It's the high diver. Tanika Dawn!* Rapid-fire memories came flooding forth. The casino high dive. The late night trampoline accident. Pookie never actually saw Tanika after the day of the accident, and while he was in the Center, he found it easy to be mad at her. Real easy. He was mad at her for falling into the hole. Mad at her for having an aunt that would actually make them shut down *Catch Some Air, Dude!* trampoline park. Mad at her for being responsible for sending him back to the Center.

But when he saw Tanika standing there in that hard white cast, he realized that she had probably not done a single dive since that fateful night. Not even a cartwheel, for that matter. And though he'd never been told, Pookie just knew, deep down, that diving was her life. He also knew, a little bit deeper down, that *he* was the one in charge that night. *He* was the one that had ignored Uncle Albert's warning. *He* was the one that had let her onto the trampolines.

Pookie decided he better stay away from Tanika. He turned back toward the first table when a hand landed on his shoulder and spun him around. "So what's it gonna be, new kid?"

"Huh?" said Pookie.

"Whatcha' gonna do after school? You need to do something. Gotta have balance, especially at a new school. You know what they say about all work and no play. So what's it gonna be? Flag football? You look like you could grow into a real bruiser. By the way," he said, holding out his hand. "I'm Trigger."

"Well," said Pookie, hiking up his books and twisting his wrist around for a sideways handshake. "I like diving."

"Diving?!" said Trigger. "That's random. I do happen to know a diver here, though. Tanika Dawn. Apparently she's pretty good, too. She trains over at Elite Prep after school."

"Elite Prep?" Pookie said. "Why?"

"I dunno," he said. "Probably because they're the closest school with diving boards." Trigger pushed his glasses up on his nose. "Anyway, from what I hear, Elite is sort of selective. The coach is supposed to be real good. Produced a bunch of champions over the years including Tanika." He took a step back and gave Pookie the once over. "You should think about soccer. I can see you now, zig-zagging down the field like a little bolt of white lightning. Besides, no guarantee they'll let you on those diving boards. They're pretty selective."

"What do you mean *selective*?"

"Well, they only let their own students on the boards. Either that, or you need to have already proven yourself somehow."

"Well how the heck are you supposed to prove yourself if-"

"Yo. Yo. Yo," Cross came up from behind, grabbed Trigger's belt loop with one hand, and Pookie's with the other. "If it isn't my two favorite people. My brotha's from otha motha's," He yanked them back and forth and knocked them into each other.

"You know this slice o' white bread?" said Trigger, his glasses tipping to one side.

"Well duh!" said Cross. "We're only living together! Pookie's my home boy from the Center. And now he's sharing a room with me here in Bridgeton, not to mention foster parents!"

"Hey!" said Pookie, as his books started to shake loose. "Let go!"

"You mean" said Trigger, "the Richardsons took in another-"

"Yup," said Cross, letting go of the boys' belt loops. Pookie lunged forward, almost dropping his books in the process. "They just moved him in. We're even building out an extra room in the basement. Man, Trigg, you should see this kid run. Fastest thing you ever saw. We just *gotta* get him out on the court this year."

"That's all we need," said Trigger. "Another white shrimp like you. I was trying to tell him about Soccer, Cross. And Track. And Flag Football."

"My little brother!" Cross slapped Pookie on the back, accidentally knocking his textbooks onto the ground with a thud. "An athlete in the making."

Pookie didn't hear any of this last bit. He didn't bend down to pick up his books, either. Instead, he stared straight ahead at the big grassy hill beyond the trees. The perfect place for a thousand cartwheels in a row. And maybe a back flip at the end.

CHAPTER TWENTY-TWO

Tanika Dawn stepped up onto the bus.

Pookie stood in the very back of the line. He started following her back at the *After School Activity* sign-up tables, the moment she announced, "I'm off to diving practice!" to her friends. He followed her first to the water fountain, and then to her locker, where she grabbed a duffel bag marked USA Diving. Now, he was following her onto a bus.

He knew he could get in trouble. After all, he was supposed to walk home from school with Cross after the Activity Sign-Ups. But, truth of the matter was, there was simply nothing more important in the world than this. He walked down the center aisle. The seats were filled, two kids to a side, all the way to the back of the bus, except for one: the seat next to Tanika.

"Kid, take a seat!" yelled the driver as the bus lurched forward.

Pookie practically fell into the seat next to Tanika.

"What the?" Tanika instantly recognized Pookie. "You're that kid from the-!" She pushed herself up and looked around, like she was expecting there to be hidden camera somewhere. Then she sat down again. "That kid from last summer!"

"Can I sign your cast?" he said, lost for any other words.

"No," said Tanika quickly. And then, "Yeah, I guess," she sighed.

"How you gonna practice with a cast?" he said as he reached into the spring of his spiral notebook, pinched out a blue pen, and removed the cap.

"Stretching, abdominal work," she said, resting her cast on the seat back. "Watching Olympic videos. I can't get in the water, but I gotta keep coming to the pool. What are you doing here, anyway? I thought you were an orphan."

"I got adopted," said Pookie as he drew a little squiggle to test the ink, "by Cross' family in Bridgeton."

"Cross' family?! The Richardsons? Well, you know you're a walker, right? This bus is for students that live way out in the country. I'm only on it because they make a special stop at Elite Prep."

Pookie replaced the pen cap, looked Tanika in the eye, and said, "I'm going to dive practice with you. Scoot over a little, will ya'?"

"Kid," said Tanika as she searched her cast for Pookie's signature. "This is Elite Prep. As in, they're all r-r-r-rich there. They're not gonna let you on the boards. Heck, you'd be lucky to get onto the deck."

Pookie held up his finger and pointed to her wrist. Then he pulled his finger slowly downward across the cast. He dragged beneath Trigger's forearm quote, *Be not afraid of greatness.* He drew an imaginary circle around Danielle's elbow quote, *The show must go on!* Then, he moved his finger around to the back of the cast.

POOKIE, it said. And instead of O's, there were two little eyeballs and a zig-zag mouth beneath them. "Pookie's my name," he said. "Don't wear it out."

CHAPTER TWENTY-THREE

"Elite is a private team," said Sally McSally. The thin-jawed secretary never looked up from her desk when she delivered the news to Pookie. "We're not taking any new divers." It sounded eerily familiar to Pookie: the sentence, her snooty tone. "I'm sure you understand."

"Well, is there an open session or something?" said Pookie. "I used to go down to the Y and dive off the boards. I was getting real good, too. Last summer I even almost did a double fl-"

"Sally, would you call Mrs. Littleneck and ask her if she's sent in her monthly-," a man with thinning hair and a brown moustache stepped in from the back room.

Pookie hiked his textbooks higher onto his hip.

"Who's this?" said the man.

"Not sure," said Sally McSally as she peered over her spectacles. "But he's rather insistent about using our diving boards."

"Yes, well you see it works a little differently at Elite," the man said. "This pool is not open to the public. We can't just allow *anyone off the streets* to just-"

Pookie followed the man's gaze downward. Sure enough, his shirt was wrinkled and untucked, and the hand-me-down pants from Cross were wadded up at the crotch. He looked back up at the man and remembered something – the glob of mustard! The dude from last summer! Coach Straw Hat! Brittany and the gang's coach!

"Hey!" yelled Pookie, thrilled by the coincidence. "You're that guy that was teaching those kid divers this summer, and I came over with my Uncle Albert and-" Pookie stopped mid-sentence, suddenly recalling how that day ended in a horrible bellyflop.

The man's face went blank, "Well you see, we have liability issues that prevent us from allowing untrained athletes from-"

As the man boringly blathered on, Pookie stared out the window at three long blue planks: two one-meters and a three-meter. Flailing swimmer-limbs churned up the water beneath them, while Tanika sat on the end of the closest board, swinging her feet back and forth. "For Pete's sake," Pookie interrupted the man. Those boards aren't even being used. I could get on 'em right now and show you my moves. Come on coach, what's the big deal? Move the swimmers. I'll be careful, coach. I'll be careful!"

Coach Dickerson looked at his secretary in mild horror while saying to Pookie, "Look, I'm sure Ms. McSally has already informed you that there are only two ways to access these diving boards. *One* is if you are selected to be a member of the Elite Preparatory School team. You were *not selected* last summer. The other is if you are a student here taking a P.E. class and-"

"I AM a student here!" Pookie turned red as soon as he told the lie. "Look!" He yanked the textbooks forward. *Algebra* slipped loose, and the entire stack tumbled from his hands. "Look, I know you don't believe me, but since you last saw me, I got adopted and-"

"Adopted?" said Sally McSally. Then she made a funny sound.

"You mean that man at the Y wasn't your father?" said Coach Davidson.

"No," said Pookie. "I just told you - he was my Uncle Albert."

“What’s your last name, son?” said Sally McSally as she clicked onto her computer.

Pookie hadn’t considered that the dive office would have its own student database. “Ah, never mind,” he said, not wanting to be caught. He scooped up the big mess of books, swung the bundle onto his left hip, opened the door, and slammed it behind him. The blinds flapped violently against the glass, jingling a bunch of happy little prep school bells.

CHAPTER TWENTY-FOUR

Pookie bobbled down the steps of the poolside hut. Then he stepped around the corner and lugged his books up onto a raised director chair.

"That's Coach Dickerson's chair," said a skinny girl with straight blonde hair. "You better get those books off before he comes out."

"Well, where'm I supposed to put 'em?" said Pookie.

"Here," said Tanika, hopping off the board. "Put them back here." Tanika walked to an opening behind the hut. "This is the old trampoline pit," she said. "We're not using it right now."

"Cool, it's a built-in," Pookie dropped to his knees. He put his books on the corner ledge and ran his palm across the surface. "Yeah, there's a buncha holes in it." He made a fist and pounded the edge. "Still good, though. "He rolled into the sagging center and hopped to his feet. "Still bounce-able." As he launched into a bounce, the rusty old springs made a creaking noise.

"You better get off!" shouted Brittany, pulling at her purple bathing suit.

"What?!" said Pookie as he flailed his arms. "I can't hear you!"

"See that spotting rig over your head?" said Tanika.

"Snowboard karate chop combo!" yelled Pookie, throwing his legs out to one side.

"Pookie, stop!" yelled Tanika.

Pookie fell to the mat with a thud and a sigh. He crossed his arms behind his head and lowered himself onto his back.

"You best settle down," said Tanika. "See the spotting rig up there?"

Pookie put his hand up to shield the afternoon sun. There was a beam way up high, with ropes hanging diagonally downward. The ropes came together at two clips, one on either side of a red canvas belt.

"That's how we learn new dives," said Tanika. "We get into the belt and Coach Dickerson suspends us in mid-air while learning a new trick. You can add a somersault, a half somersault, or whatever. It's much better to try new dives on the belt before you take them up to the boards."

"Bet I could climb up there and bring it down," said Pookie. "Wanna see?"

"Dooon't," whined Brittany. "We can't use it until we get a new trampoline. You're gonna get us in trouble."

"I wish Elite would hurry up and get a new tramp already," said Tanika. She turned to walk back out onto the deck. "I'm over it."

"I know, right?" said Brittany, twirling her hair.

"Do you always agree with whatever she says?" said Pookie.

"No," said Brittany, picking at her suit.

Pookie laid back down and thrust his hips into the air. The springs creaked. One. Two. Three-

"You better cut it out," said Brittany.

"Brittany!" Tanika yelled out from the deck. "We're starting group stretch."

"Coming!" yelled Brittany as she scooted out to the deck.

Pookie laid back on the sagging trampoline. He looked up at the belt and imagined being inside of it, grabbing his knees and squeezing himself into a tight little ball. He imagined himself flipping, over and over again like a pinwheel. He imagined flipping until his face caved in. Flipping until his hair caught on fire. Flipping until-

Roooaaarrrr! A cyborg roared inside of his pocket. He pulled out his cell phone. A text. *So you got a cell phone, huh, kid? Good job. The Richardsons gave me your number. I'm on my way back to Jersey. Hope to see you when I get there. I will text you in a couple of days, after I check into a hotel. -Uncle Albert.*

Pookie rolled off the trampoline, hoisted himself up, and started toward the deck. Roooaaaarrr! The cyborg went off in his hand. Another text, this time from Cross. *Where the heck are you?!?*

On deck, the bright blue gym mat was unfolded beside the diving board. Brittany and a small, perfect boy were sitting, side by side, legs out in front. Behind them, Tanika and an older blonde girl pushed down on their backs.

"No cell phones!" Coach Dickerson barked into the air.

Pookie startled and looked over at the director's chair. Coach Dickerson was sitting there against the hut with his legs crossed. A woman with a thousand silver bracelets and a wave of rigid, grey-blonde hair stood beside him.

CHAPTER TWENTY-FIVE

"You!" said Coach Dickerson, pointing to Pookie as clicked off his cell phone. "Get over here."

Pookie walked over with his head hung low. He stood in front of Coach Dickerson, ready to be kicked off the deck. After all, he'd already racked up three punishable offenses: (1) being an imposter, (2) bouncing on the trampoline, and (3) using his cell phone.

"Mrs. Kadillak here just gave me this silver money clip," said Coach Dickerson as he lifted a hairy, tanned leg and crossed it over the other. "I quite like it. What do you think?"

"It's very nice," said Pookie.

"Yes," he said, twirling it around in his fingers. "I think it *is* very nice, too. I like gifts," he said. "I think everybody likes gifts. Don't you?"

"Brittany! Kirk!" Mrs. Kadillak interrupted, scrolling her fingers into a wave. "Have a good practice, my little angels!"

"Okay," Brittany and Kirk mumbled into their knees.

"Now, if I could only keep this thing filled," said Coach Dickerson, fingering the money clip.

"Tell me about it," said Mrs. Kadillak, laughing.

Coach Dickerson stretched out his leg until it was just inches from Pookie's face. He pointed his feet but stretched his toes up and back. Then he spread them so that his toes were fanned out like peacock feathers. "Nice, Doug," giggled Mrs. Kadillak. A moment later, he creepily flattened his feet and curled his toes downward. "You always did have the best toepoint, Doug," said Mrs. Kadillak, admiring Coach Dickerson's hairy feet.

"Well I better go," said Pookie awkwardly. "I'll bring my bathing suit tomorrow." "Look, kid," Coach Dickerson relaxed his feet and rested his hands on his knee. "You and I both know you're not a student at Elite Prep. I mean, look at your clothes. Look at your shoes."

Mrs. Kadillak stood by, stifling a giggle.

Pookie looked down at himself. Too big pants. Ratty old shoes. Cross said he was gonna use white-out on them, but he hadn't gotten to it since he was so busy building out the basement with Mr. Richardson.

"And even if you *were* a student here," said Coach Dickerson. "I don't think you're the right – uh, how can I put this pleasantly – the right body type. I suggest you find another sport."

Pookie felt like he'd been kicked in the stomach.

He looked over at the mat and stared at the team.

Tanika stood in the corner of the mat, cast in the air, rotating from side to side. Her face was a statue. Her body was a rock. She stared straight ahead in a cold stone focus.

Brittany, the perfect little Barbie Doll, hopped up and down beside her.

Kirk, a Ken Doll in a Speedo with brown wavy hair, wobbled on his tippy toes, arms, hands, and fingers, reaching up to the blue sky.

And in the far corner, there was a curvy older girl, lying flat on her back, pumping her legs above as if she was riding a bicycle.

"Will there be anything else?" Coach Dickerson said to Pookie. Then he sighed and looked at Mrs. Kadillak, who was busy examining her fingernails.

This was the last straw of the day. Getting his body bashed by a tree branch was one thing. But getting his dreams dashed by an evil, straw-hat-wearing adult was enough to send him over the edge. Pookie turned away and ran across the pool deck. He ran past the swimming lanes, through the main gate, out into the fancy car parking lot, under the big *Elite Preparatory School* archway, and onto the country road.

Pookie's head and neck were filled with cotton. His legs were like two wooden planks. Unable to think, scream, cry, or anything else, he turned a cartwheel. And then another. And then a third. The hot, grey asphalt scorched his hands, but he just kept spinning anyway.

CHAPTER TWENTY-SIX

"Look who I found cartwheeling down the road," said Aunt BeeBee, strumming her red fingernails against her Coupe de Ville steering wheel.

"Aunt BeeBee!" Tanika opened the passenger side door and slid in to the seat beside her beloved aunt. "What are you doing here? Where's my mom?"

"Your momma and gramma are busy today, child," said Aunt BeeBee. "Apparently bowls of chicken pastry are flying out that door."

"Pookie! What are *you* doing here?!" Tanika craned her head around to look into the back seat. "Where the heck did you go?! Oh, and hey, we've got your books."

The passenger-side back door swung open, and the curvy blonde from dive practice spun inside and plopped Pookie's books down into the empty space between them. "Mustn't forget these," she said in a sing-song voice. Then she leaned over, rolled her eyes, and whispered, "though if it were up to me, I woulda' left the algebra book behind. Math is such a yawn, don'tcha think?"

"Well, I uh-," but before Pookie could answer, the girl popped in some earbuds and started bouncing her bleach-blonde head from side to side. The strong scent of chlorine wafted across the seat, mixing in with leather. Pookie inhaled deeply. These smells were good. Very good.

"That's Laura," said Tanika. "She just got shipped down from Canada. She doesn't go to Bridgeton, though. She goes to Egg Harbor Middle. She's staying at our farm until her mom moves down."

"I got second at the trampoline nationals, you know," said Laura, pulling out her earbuds and snapping her gum like a tiny machine gun. "But then my coach was bouncing around in the dark one night and got hurt so the program got shut down." She put her earbuds back in. "Ooooh! I just love this song!"

"Is it okay if we *not* talk about trampolines for a second?" said Aunt BeeBee. "It's really starting to work my nerves."

"Well if we don't talk about trampolines and diving," said Tanika. "What else is there to talk about?"

"Well," said Aunt BeeBee, "we could talk about what happened on Peanut Pier last summer."

The car engine hummed along, low and smooth.

Tanika poked a pencil beneath her cast, eraser-side first.

"I would like to climb high in a tree!" Laura sang along to her music. "I could be happy! I could be happy!"

Pookie sent a text: *Hi Cross I'm on my way home now.* Then he scrolled down to read Uncle Albert's text again. He could hardly wait to see Uncle Albert. He thought of Coach Dickerson and his big freaky toes and the money clip. Then he thought of the saggy old trampoline behind the hut and how they could really use an upgrade.

And just when all of these thoughts were swirling around like little fishes in his brain, the Coup de' Ville went over a speed bump, and an idea popped loose. "I've got it!" said Pookie, as his thumbs assumed the texting position: *Uncle Albert do you still have the trampolines because the diving team needs one. I want to get on the team and I think this is the way how.*

CHAPTER TWENTY-SEVEN

One Week Later

"Suck it in, Grace," Coach Dickerson yelled from the trampoline pit. "Brittany, watch Pookie's dive. Make sure he sucks in his gut and points his toes." Then he turned back toward Laura, who was standing in the middle of the trampoline, belted up with her arms wrapped in ropes.

"You heard him, Grace. Suck it in," said Brittany, "and point your toes."

Pookie stood in place, waiting for Laura to do her trampoline trick. He hated that they called him Grace. It was just plain mean. "Again," said Coach Dickerson. He pulled the ropes, catapulting Laura into the air. At the top, she slapped her knees and squeezed into a tuck. "Hup!" yelled Coach

Dickerson after the first somersault. She kicked her legs up into the air, reached her arms back toward the trampoline mat, touched it, and then brought her legs around to vertical. "You people are whack-jobs," she said as she landed, "I mean, who the heck lands head first?"

"This is diving, Laura," said Coach Dickerson. "Not trampoline. Not gymnastics. Diving. Oh, and by the way, that was perfect."

"Well thanks, Coach," said Laura. "Hey Pookster," she yelled. "This trampoline kicks some serious A! Thanks for hooking us up. That other one was saggin' lower than my grandpa's butt!"

Back on the diving boards, Pookie clasped his arm around his belly and took an awkward step down the one-meter board.

"Look natural," said Kirk. "They'll laugh you off the deck if you walk like that in the meet."

"I'm trying!" Pookie took a half-step. Then he stopped to tug at his bunched-up nylon Speedo.

"C'mon, Grace," said Brittany. "Walk down the board like you're walking down the street. You *can* walk normal, can't you?"

"I *am* walking normal!" yelled Pookie. But really, Pookie had no idea how to walk normal. All he knew was how to run away from the bullies - and do cartwheels. He took another step.

When he finally made it to the end of the wobbling board, Pookie jumped up with both feet and then stomped them down hard. Too hard. Then he flailed his arms toward the water. Again, too hard.

It was supposed to be a simple forward dive, but instead, his hands grazed the surface and his legs flew over his head.

FWAAK! The back of his feet slapped against the water. It stung and burned and Pookie blew a jillion scream bubbles before swimming to the surface. He sputtered to the edge, red-faced and red-heeled.

"Interesting," Brittany echoed through the concrete gutter. "More than a dive but not quite a flip! What was it, Pookie? A three-quarters?"

"Jesus, Grace, your feet are like this!" Coach Dickerson stomped over to the edge, kicked off his sandals, and fanned out his hairy toes. "It's a good thing your uncle donated that trampoline because otherwise...well, let's just put it this way: not pretty!"

"Oh my god!" yelled Tanika from the stretching mat, where she stared at the I-Pad video monitor. "Xing Yao and his synchro partner were just about to do a 109C. His partner balked and he kept going, and, well, they failed the dive. Ouch!"

"What meet are you watching" said Coach Dickerson, stepping over her on his way back to the trampoline.

"FINA Grand Prix in Fort Lauderdale," she said.

"What the heck is a 109C?" yelled Pookie.

"Duhhh!" said Brittany.

"It's a front four-and-a-half tuck," said Tanika. "You can figure it out pretty easy. The first number stands for the direction. One is forward, two is back, three is reverse, four is inward, and five is a twister. The next number stands for the number of rotations. Each number represents a half somersault. So a 101 is a forward dive, a 102 is a flip, a 103 is a one-and-a-half, and so on. The letters are the positions. A,B,C,D stand for straight, pike, tuck, and twisting."

"Oh," said Pookie. "That's sorta complicated."

"Don't worry about it, Grace," said Coach Dickerson. "You just keep working on that 911 of yours. The ambulance will be here to get you anytime."

CHAPTER TWENTY-EIGHT

"In field hockey this weekend," Principal Kimple said over the loudspeaker. "The Bulldogs played a great game but were defeated by Country Day Middle School. Final score: Bridgeton Bulldogs 1. Country Day Middle School 3."

In the back of Mrs. Polk's classroom, Pookie's heart beat in anticipation of after-school dive practice. He couldn't think of anything else these days. Ever since he overheard Doug Dickerson consoling Tanika about not being able to dive in the upcoming U.S. Diving Invitational, he was obsessed.

"In soccer this weekend," Principal Kimple continued. "The Bridgeton Bulldogs defeated Egg Harbor Township. Final score: Bridgeton Bulldogs 2. Egg Harbor Township: 1."

Pookie sat up straight at his desk and sucked in his belly. He hadn't quite met the difficulty requirements to compete. He needed eleven whole dives, not his measly three. But he just *had* to compete with the U.S. Age Group Divers. After the Invitational would be the Zone meet. And after the Zone meet came Nationals. Pookie squeezed his eyes shut and curled his toes down into his old sneakers, thinking about the dives he had to learn in order to get to Nationals: the inward dive, the reverse dive, the reverse flip, the back one-and-a-half, and the list went on.

His palms were sweating. He never used to be afraid, but after the last two wipe-outs - one ending in welts and another ending in two black eyes - fear had crept up and slowed his progress to a crawl.

"In flag football," announced Principal Kimple. "Bridgeton Bulldogs 20. Cherry Hill 0. Way to go, Bulldogs!"

In the back of her classroom, Tanika doodled a diver onto her frayed cast. "Hockey, football, soccer," Tanika sighed under her breath. "That's all we ever hear about around here."

Tanika wasn't too thrilled about the upcoming meet. Fact was, Laura Dash had transferred her trampoline skills to the diving boards so quickly that she had a list as difficult as Tanika's. And because the girls trained together and even *lived* together, Tanika had to clap, smile, and hug her. But deep down, she wasn't pleased at all.

"Enjoy your moment, Laura," she mumbled to herself. "And don't act *too* proud, girl. Cuz this cast is gonna be off real soon."

CHAPTER TWENTY-NINE

"Ladies and gentlemen," said the emcee of the Wendy Wyland U.S. Diving Invitational. "This morning, the Twelve-and-Under boys will be competing on the one-meter springboard, and the Twelve-and-Under girls will be competing on the three-meter springboard. Our first diver is Pookie Jameson doing a 101B. Forward dive in the pike position."

"Go Pook!" yelled Uncle Albert from somewhere the bleachers.

"You got it, Pookie!" yelled Laura Dash as she squeezed water from her chamois.

"Walk normal," Pookie said to himself. "Stand up on the end of the board. Reach. Bend. Look. Stretch. Point your toes." He walked with his back straight, trying to remember everything he'd ever been told. But there were too many things. It was all becoming a big jumble.

Left foot, right foot, left foot, right foot. At the final row of rivets, he lifted his left knee, hopped to the end with both feet together, and swung his arms. With his eyes on the water's surface, he touched the backs of his feet, straightened his body, and stretched with all of his might.

Splash! He swam up to the surface quickly, just in time to hear the scores. "Five. Five. Five. Five and a half. Six."

"That'll work," Pookie sputtered to the pool's edge, hoisting himself from the water.

Laura Dash, standing beside the three-meter board, gave him a nod and a big thumbs up. Then she smiled, blew him a kiss, and lifted a pointed toe up behind her curvy backside. Pookie shook the water from his head.

In a split second, Laura's smile disappeared. She turned around to face the three meter board, stretched her arms out to the sides, and closed them overhead. Once, twice, three times,-"

"Kirk Kadillak," said the announcer. "102B. Forward dive in the pike position."

Kirk Kadillak, child star of the Elite Prep diving team, had been training with Coach Dickerson since he was six. And though he consistently slid through the water with perfect toes and no splash, his optional dives were getting weak.

"Awards please," said the announcer.

The judges flipped open their black-and-white score cards.

"Seven. Eight. Eight. Seven-and-a-half. Seven," said the emcee. The audience whistled and whooped. "Way to go, Kirk!" said Pookie as Kirk Kadillak walked over to him on the deck. "Sevens and eights! Jeez Louise!"

"Thanks," he said flatly. "I always get that."

Pookie and Kirk stood side by side as the other boys took their turns. Mostly forward dives. A few back dives. A couple of inward dives. There were lots of splats and funky, flailing feet.

Tanika Dawn sat at the scoring table, writing down the judge's scores, adding them up, and passing the sheet along to Mrs. Diggleberry. Mrs. Diggleberry sat next to her, multiplying the sum of scores by the degree of difficulty.

"On the three meter board," said the announcer. "Laura Dash. 401B. Inward dive in the pike position."

CHAPTER THIRTY

With a face as serious as the school librarian, Laura Dash adjusted the fulcrum and put her hair behind her ears. She threw her chamois down and walked to the end of the board. As the board wobbled to a standstill, she turned around backwards, put her arms out to the side, and took a deep breath.

"Go Laura!" yelled Pookie. "Rip it!"

Tanika looked up from the score table as Laura lifted her arms, sprung into the air, touched her toes, and dropped, in a straight line, three meters down to the water.

"Oh my!" said Mrs. Diggleberry. "Where did *she* come from? So strong! And elegant! Such a rare combination!"

"They shipped her down to train with us at Elite," Tanika said as she scribbled down the scores, "She was a trampoline star."

"She's quite big," said Mrs. Diggleberry. "Are we *sure* she should be in the Twelve-and-Under competition?"

"Good point," said Tanika. "Someone should check her date of birth."

Pookie watched as Laura Dash scooped up her yellow chamois and walk over to the judging panel. Without taking his eyes off the diving well, Coach Dickerson whispered some quick tips. Laura nodded and tippy-toed to a place just beyond the bleachers. There, she laid out her towel and popped in her earbuds.

"Brittany Kadillak," said the announcer. "401B. Inward dive in the pike position."

There was a smattering of applause. Without a single noticeable improvement, Brittany Kadillak had remained the darling of Jersey Diving since she was five years old. Since Tanika Dawn was one age group ahead of Brittany and in a class by herself, Brittany was still able to take home the gold at most local meets.

"Go Brittany!" yelled Mrs. Kadillak. "You got it, Princess!"

Brittany Kadillak stepped to the end of the three-meter board, turned around, and prepared for take-off. A quick spin of the arms later, she popped her hips back, touched her toes, and stretched for the water. Halfway through the drop, her legs and toes, locked and pointed, twisted a bit to one side.

"Awwww," said the crowd. When she popped up to the surface, everybody applauded. "Four. Six. Eight. Four. Seven. Four."

"Make up your minds, judges," sighed Tanika as she scribbled scores into the row of boxes.

"What the heck?" said Pookie. "Sevens and Fours on the same dive?"

"Oh, they don't know *what* to give her sometimes," said Kirk Kadillak. "You never know when she might have another melt-down."

CHAPTER THIRTY-ONE

Pookie was at the urinal when he heard his name.

"Pookie Jameson, 403C. Inward one-and-a-half somersaults in the tuck position."

"Oh no!" He said as he tied the string on his Speedo. "Oh no! Oh nooo!" He pumped his arms and slapped his feet in fast motion across the tiles of the locker room floor, then across the hot, wet deck.

"Pookie," said the emcee. "It's okay. We'll wait."

Pookie slowed down a little but continued to goofily pump his arms.

"Don't hurt yourself," said the announcer.

Pookie leaned back and marched, sorta like Mr. Peanut at the pier.

The crowd chuckled.

Pookie straightened himself out. As he passed by the score table and noticed that Tanika was holding up a single finger. *One thought,* she mouthed.

He took a deep breath, slowed his pace, and stepped toward the ladder.

"One thought," he said quietly to himself. It was short-hand for the advice she'd given him before the meet. *Remember Pookie,* she'd told him during the warm-up, *Focus on one thing about a dive, otherwise your brain will get all mixed up. Pick one thought and zone in on it. Your body will do the rest."*

"What'd you say I was doing?" shouted Pookie.

"An inward one-and-a-half," said the announcer. "Tuck."

The crowd laughed a little harder and then fell silent.

Pookie walked out to the end of the board and turned around. "Throw over the board," he said to himself.

He bobbed with his heels hanging off the edge, his eyes opened wide in pre-dive terror. Throwing over the board was the *single scariest thought* anyone could have. But it was essential to make the rotation. "Throw over the board," Pookie whispered to himself while pumping his arms and taking a deep breath.

In the air, Pookie's arms threw down in front of him as planned, but his rear end had a different notion. Back and down he went, away from the board.

"Arrrruuuuggggghhh," he squeezed his knees harder than ever before. He was only about a foot off the surface when he passed the somersault point. He snuck his hands out above his head and thrust his feet up into the air.

"Awards please," said the announcer as he swam to the gutter.

"Five. Five. Five-and-a-half. Five-and-a-half. Five."

"Meh," said Pookie, blowing bubbles into the water. "Coulda' been better." He got out of the water and turned around to watch the next diver.

"Kirk Kadillak," said the announcer. "104C. Double somersault, tuck position."

"Go Kirk!" yelled random people from the crowd. "You got it!"

"Oh, this is his *faaavorite,*" said Mrs. Kadillak. She happened to say this just as the applause was dying down, so her voice carried across the deck and up to the diving board.

"Mom," Kirk shook his head angrily as he turned the fulcrum.

He walked down the board, hopped into a hurdle, and swung his arms back up to the top. The dive started out okay: a nice, solid somersault with plenty of height. But then he started to unravel. First one leg, which basically put him into a can-opener, and then the next, and then, FWAAAAK!

"Awards, please," said the announcer.

Kirk swam to the edge with no expression, just a wet wave of brown hair pasted across his forehead.

"Three. Two. Two. One-and-a-Half. Two."

"Wa-wahh," said Kirk, as he took his place beside Pookie.

"Well *that* sure bit the big one."

"Kirk and Pookie," said Coach Dickerson from his seat at the end of the judges panel. "Come over here for a second, guys."

CHAPTER THIRTY-TWO

"What's up next, Kirk?" said Coach Dickerson.

"Gainer," said Kirk, quietly. "Reverse one-and-a-half."

"Okay, Kirk. You've got this," said Coach Dickerson. "Just remember. Slow in your hurdle, reach, and power through your legs."

"Back-and-a-half," said Pookie.

"One sec," said Coach Dickerson, holding up his hand. On the three meter board, Laura Dash bobbed backward on the end, preparing for take-off. "Reach!" Coach Dickerson said quietly to himself as he twisted his body in the chair. Laura rocketed upward and her legs, straight as an arrow, raised up in front of her face. Then she wrapped her arms around them, and spun around twice. "Hup,"

Coach Dickerson said quietly, and she laid back and stretched for the water, going in with hardly a splash.

"Yessss!" said Coach Dickerson. "Now that's a back two-and-a-half pike!"

"Holy mother of-" said Pookie.

"Pookie, did you see how she stood up and jumped with all of her might?" Coach Dickerson said as he fumbled with his score card.

"Uh huh," said Pookie.

"Well," he pulled open the Seven Card and held it up in the air. "That's what you have to do on your back-and-a-half. Reach strong. Go for it as hard and as you can. The reason why you've been smacking on this is dive is because you always hold back. And that throws off your spots. In fact, you don't even get to your spots because it throws off *everything.*"

Laura Dash scooped up her chamois and trotted over to Coach Davidson.

"Nice, Laura, what's next?" said Coach Dickerson.

"Double out," she said.

"Okay," said Coach Dickerson. "Steady hurdle, reach up and-"

The boys turned to walk away. But as they were walking away, Laura rolled up her chamois and flicked it at Pookie's behind. "Hey," she said, smacking him gently in the Speedo. “Nice save on that inward.”

“Holy crap,” said Pookie, blushing. “She saw it!”

“So?” said Kirk.

“I dunno,” he said. “I just thought that - well, she’s so good and all. Why would she pay attention to-”

“You’re weird,” said Kirk.

“So?” said Pookie. He raised his arms and closed his eyes to visualize his next dive, the back-and-a-half tuck. But every time he tried to picture the dive, he kept seeing last week’s wipe-out. The smack that hurt so bad that he actually cried. The one where welts were all over his back for two whole days. “Single thought,” he said, opening his eyes. “Go for it.”

“Huh?” said Kirk.

“Nothing.”

CHAPTER THIRTY-THREE

"Four. Seven-and-a-half. Three. Four. Three. "Interference!" yelled Brittany as she swam to the side in a panic. "Laura Dash was dancing and I heard her sing something about climbing in a tree and it distracted me! I want a do-over!"

"Ladies and gentlemen," said the announcer. "Please stand by."

"Sorry," said Laura as she inhaled into another machine gun bubblegum snap. "I didn't know I was singing out loud."

"In all my years," Coach Sandy Hardnail, who sat in the judges chair next to Coach Dickerson. "I have *never* seen such a primadonna. Seriously, somebody has *got* to do something. There are no do-overs. This isn't a-"

“Interference,” said the announcer calmly. “Brittany Kadillak, you may go again. 203A. Back one-and-a-half somersaults, straight position.”

Coach Dickerson shrugged his shoulders.

“Go again, honey!” yelled Mrs. Kadillak from beside the emcee.

Brittany marched it up the ladder with an angry red face. She stomped out to the end of the board, glared down at the deck, and stuck her tongue out at Laura Dash. Then she turned around, and without giving herself a chance to even *have* a single thought, she started the dive. She bobbed on the end once, jumped up, whipped her head and neck back, and threw her arms down. “Aaaaahhhhh!” she screamed through the entire first somersault. And then, at the moment she should have looked back and dove in head first, she bunched up into a ball and flipped over to her feet. Well, actually, her hands and knees.

“What the-” said Pookie. “She did a double!”

“Sorta,” said Kirk. “Actually it was a midair meltdown.”

“Failed dive,” said the announcer.

"Pookie Jameson," said the announcer. 203C. Back one-and-a-half tuck."

Pookie stood backward on the end of the board. His back tingled in the place where the welts used to be.

"Come on, Pookie!" yelled Laura Dash. "You got this."

"Go Pook," said Tanika. "Shred it, boy."

"Nail it, Pookster!" yelled Uncle Albert.

Pookie shimmied his heels off the edge of the board, and the pool went silent. He stared at the tiny little Duraflex tag and put his arms to the side. Then he bobbed his arms. While he was bobbing, he thought about the welts. *No!* Thought about the smack. *No!* Thought about the million wipeouts and accidents and eggs and rocks and tree branches.

No! No! No! And then, in a single instant, all of the voices and all of the racing thoughts in his mixed-up little brain shrunk into one little dot when he remembered: *single thought.*

"Go for it," he said. And with the force of a thousand cartwheels, Pookie Jameson reached and jumped. At the top, he lifted his knees up past the Duraflex tag and up over his head. He squeezed his legs into his chest with a firm grip, and-

"Kick!" Coach Dickerson whispered at the judge's panel, twisting in his chair.

Pookie kicked, looked back, and reached for the water.

"Yessss!" said Tanika, making a fist and pulling it into her chest as Pookie plopped into the water. One foot was pointed, and one was flat, but still, it was solid. "Right on, Pookie," she smiled, blew on her pencil tip, and pointed it at the first box.

Five feet beneath the surface of the water, Pookie was not sure what happened. The dive actually felt good. Really good. In fact, it didn't hurt at all! He turned a flip in the water and swam up as quickly as he could.

"Six. Six. Five. Five-and-a-half. Six," said the announcer.

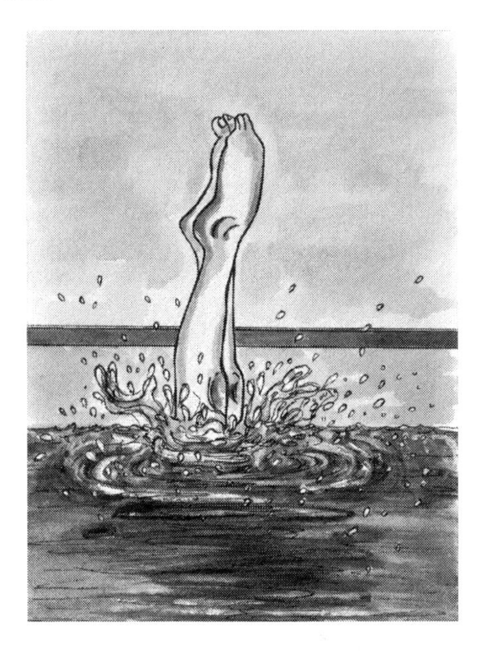

CHAPTER THIRTY-FOUR

Pookie slapped his feet against the hot, wet deck as he ran-walked over toward Uncle Albert in the bleachers.

"Pssst," whispered Tanika. "You've come a long way from those carnival trampolines, kid." She poked her fist out from beneath the scoring table. "Nice full list. Keep it up and you could make Nationals."

"Nationals?" He reached out, made a fist, and bumped Tanika's knuckles.

"Nice job, Pookie," said Mrs. Diggleberry in the seat next to her.

"Kirk Kadillak," said the announcer. "303C. Reverse one-and-a-half somersaults in the tuck position."

"Go Kirk!" he said, turning to face the diving board. "You got this!"

Kirk adjusted the fulcrum and placed his hands at his sides.

The deck went dark as two cold hands covered Pookie's eyes. He ducked and whipped around. It was Laura Dash. "Shhh! Shhh!" she whispered, smiling. "You don't want to cause an *interference,* do you?"

"Uh, no," Pookie whispered. "I uh-"

"Pretty impressive performance today, Pook-a-licious," she whispered. "You know, I used to know somebody like you at the trampoline nationals. Consistent. Hard working. Dedicated."

"Kirk Kadillak," repeated the announcer. "303C. Reverse one-and-a-half somersaults in the tuck position."

Pookie and Laura turned toward the diving board. Something was weird. Dives were *never* announced twice.

"Thirty second warning, Kirk," said the announcer.

Kirk Kadillak stood, terrified yet expressionless, on the diving board.

"You got it, Kirk!" yelled Laura, bumping her bare shoulder into Pookie's.

"Come on, Kirk!" yelled Pookie, bumping back.

"Failed dive," said the announcer.

Kirk stood like a statue. His hair, now completely dry, fluttered on his forehead.

"Kirk," said the announcer. "Did you hear me? I said failed dive. Please step down."

Kirk didn't budge.

"Awkward," said Laura Dash in a sing-song voice.

"It's okay, baby!" Mrs. Kadillak said, bustling over to the ladder and reaching across the board with an arm full of silver bracelets. "C'mon down."

Pookie turned away from the embarrassing scene and continued toward the bleachers to see Uncle Albert.

"Hey kid," said Uncle Albert. "Gimme a high five!"

Pookie held up his hand. His Uncle Albert twisted his arm, yanked him into his lap, and tousled his head. "Way to go kid! I'm proud of ya'!"

"Thanks," said Pookie. "You know, that was my first full list. Eleven whole dives."

"Hey, that's great," Uncle Albert continued. "Far cry from that day at the Y, huh? I knew you were as good as these kids. That last dive was pretty fancy. What was that? A back five-and-a-half?"

"Haha!" said Pookie. "You know it was back ONE-and-a-half."

"Listen kid," Uncle Albert cupped his hand around Pookie's ear and whispered, "what I really wanna know is, who's that little cutie that keeps talkin' to ya'?"

"You mean Laura?"

"Yeah, that one," he said. "Laura Dash. She's really somethin', huh?"

"Watch her last dive," Pookie said, wriggling away. "She's doin' a Double Out!" He bounded back down the steps, scooted across the scoring table, and grabbed his towel bag.

The three-meter board made a powerful bouncing sound as he got to Coach Dickerson's side. Pookie looked up, just in time to see Laura Dash rocketing into a mind blowing front two-and-a-half with two twists.

"Eight. Eight. Eight. Seven-and-a-half. Eight," said the announcer, his voice was raised an octave higher than normal.

"Wow," said Mrs. Diggleberry. She's gotta be the only Twelve-and-Under diver in the country doing that!" The microphone was still switched on, and the audience, and the crowd, that had been getting more excited with each of Laura's dives, jumped to their feet and cheered.

"I've just been notified that Brittany Kadillak has scratched," said the announcer as the applause died down, "so that's it for today's competition. Thank you judges. Thank you divers. The results will be announced in a few minutes."

The judges bounced to their feet. Pookie stood quietly beside Coach Dickerson, waiting. He wasn't sure what he was waiting for. Maybe a debriefing? A recap? Heck, after all that work, someone's gotta say something! But Coach Dickerson just uncrossed his hairy legs and stood up.

"How'd I do, Coach?" said Pookie. As he spoke, a jeweled hand with red fingernails reached over the top of his head.

"Coach Dickerson," said Aunt BeeBee, shaking the coach's hand. "BeeBee Jackson here. Tanika Dawn's aunt. I'd like to talk to you about the Elite pool. What it is now. What it could be. I have a good trampoline source." She looked over at Uncle Albert, alone on the top bleacher bench. "And a good construction crew. In fact, last year, we built the Big Top Casino and Peanut Pier."

"Rrrrooooaar!" The cyborg inside Pookie's bag shrieked. He reached inside and grabbed it. A text from Cross: *Where the heck are you? Mr. and Mrs. R are FREAKING. You're gonna blow this thing if you keep disappearing.*

Pookie looked around the deck, inhaled a long, sweet, burning breath of chlorine, and lined up his thumbs: *I am at a dive meet. Will be home soon.* He put the phone into his bag. Then he took it out again and texted four more words: *I am a diver.*

ABOUT THE AUTHORS

Scott Upper was a member of the U.S. National Springboard and Platform Diving Team. He was awarded athletic scholarships to UCLA and the University of Minnesota, where he earned a degree in Psychology. He lives in San Francisco, California.

Jim Upper is a former college, high school, and middle school basketball coach. Later, he worked at a residential facility for "at risk kids" in New Jersey, serving as a mentor for dozens of foster children through the Youth Advocate Program. He lives in Lake Mary, Florida.